ROSE CAMPION
and the CURSE of the
DOOMSTONE

Also by **LYN GARDNER**

Rose Campion and the Stolen Secret

Olivia's First Term
Olivia Flies High
Olivia and the Movie Stars
Olivia's Enchanted Summer
Olivia and the Great Escape
Olivia's Winter Wonderland
Olivia's Curtain Call

ROSE CAMPION
and the CURSE of the DOOMSTONE

LYN GARDNER

nosy crow

First published in the UK in 2017 by Nosy Crow Ltd
The Crow's Nest, 10a Lant Street
London, SE1 1QR, UK

www.nosycrow.com

ISBN: 978 0 85763 8441

A CIP catalogue record for this book will be available from the
British Library.

Printed and bound in the UK by Clays Ltd, St. Ives Plc
Typeset by Tiger Media

Papers used by Nosy Crow are made from wood grown in
sustainable forests.

1 3 5 7 9 10 8 6 4 2

*For Ellie, Ruari, Hector and Sid.
May you have many brilliant
adventures together.*

1

Rose Campion sighed with pleasure and leaned back in her seat as the crimson stage curtains swept closed with a satisfying swish. The house lights came up, making her blink. Then the chandeliers high above the auditorium sprang back into life, shivering and sparkling like great upside-down wedding cakes, winking with crystals and brightly coloured glass. The audience began to clap, the noise and lights propelling Rose back into the real world, so that the play suddenly seemed like a fading dream slipping beyond her grasp.

"They liked it," exclaimed Aurora, turning excitedly to Effie and Rose.

"Wrong," said Rose. "They loved it – just look at them."

Rose was right. Every single plush red velvet seat in the Pall Mall Theatre had been sold, and every seat was now empty – the glittering first-night crowd had risen to their feet to acknowledge Edward's performance as Hamlet, Prince of Denmark. Even the most refined society ladies, their swan-like necks encircled by pearls and emeralds, were standing to applaud. Rose looked around the audience, all rich, modish and lustrous, as if somebody had given them all an extra polish before they came out for the evening, and thought how removed the Pall Mall was from her beloved Campion's Palace of Varieties and Wonders. It was a different world. The audience at Campion's music hall, on the wrong side of the river in Southwark, was frequently ragged and rowdy, but they always responded straight from the heart. The poised and self-conscious Pall Mall crowd seemed to be performing a role, taking their cues from each other and glancing around anxiously to check that they were doing the right thing. A first night at the Pall Mall was clearly not just about seeing a play – it was about being seen.

"He really was good, wasn't he?" said Aurora, a touch of anxiety creeping into her voice as her father took yet another solo bow. "They're not just clapping because Edward's got a title and his rags-to-riches story is so romantic?"

Rose squeezed Aurora's hand. "Of course not," she said. "They're clapping because he's a great actor."

Which he was, thought Rose – but the fact that Edward Frederick Dorset Easingford was also the new Lord Easingford was certainly not going to be a hindrance at the box office. The production had been the talk of London society as soon as it was announced. The theatre was stuffed with dukes and duchesses – most of them, Rose suspected, entirely indifferent to Shakespeare. She wished that Thomas, owner of Campion's music hall, and the man who had found her and Aurora abandoned together on his doorstep when they were just babies, was here tonight. Thomas adored Shakespeare. She also knew that the pretensions of the first-night Pall Mall crowd would have made him laugh. But although he'd had a ticket to join them, he was needed at Campion's, where the Illustrious Gandini, the stage magician known as the Great Wizard of the North, was performing later that evening and would be drawing big crowds. You didn't turn down the Great Wizard of the North when he said he wanted to perform at your music hall, even if it was with just a few days' notice.

Since he had appeared like a rabbit out of a hat just three months earlier, way down the bill at a modest music hall in the suburbs, Gandini had swiftly acquired a reputation for eccentricity. He was in huge demand in halls all across London – a demand that was fuelled by the fact that Gandini turned most offers down. Some said that he came from Italy, where he was known for the infamous bullet-catch trick in which he caught a bullet fired from a gun between his teeth. Others swore that they had seen him in Paris, where he had successfully performed the Indian rope trick. Still more said that he had been spotted in San Francisco. The approach from Gandini, asking to play Campion's tonight, had only been made five days ago, and announced the day after that. There had been hints that if Thomas was accommodating, the Illustrious Gandini might consider a longer run at Campion's. It would be a real coup – if a small hall like Campion's could attract such top-of-the-bill acts, when there was such stiff competition from the bigger, more glamorous West End halls, its future would be secure.

"Oh, Rory," sighed Effie. "Yer dad was perfect. I've never seen anyone die so beautifully."

Except for Thomas, who she held in awe, Effie shortened almost everyone's name. Rory had stuck. It suited Aurora, particularly since she had been dressing as a boy to perform the bicycle act she did with Rose. But her pleasure in the nickname ran deeper: Aurora had grown up friendless and unloved, and was delighted to have friends close enough to affectionately shorten her name.

"Yer dad was like a real prince. And it were just like his story, weren't it? That Claudius gaffer was a real smug piece of work. He was like Ed's wicked uncle, who tried to diddle 'im out of the title and them big houses. I wanted to rush up on to the stage and give 'im a right good talking to."

Rose suppressed a smile. She wondered how the Pall Mall audience would have responded if little Effie, with her sweet, heart-shaped face, untidy ditchwater-blonde hair and eyes that gleamed like moonstones, had dared to do such a thing. She loved the way Effie always said what she thought, and her enduring cheerfulness in the face of adversity: Effie's mum, Iris, was still lingering in Holloway Prison, where she was sick with consumption. Thomas and his lawyer, Mr Cherryble, had been trying to get Effie a visit to see her mother. Edward and his lawyers had been helping too, but so far in vain.

"Come on," said Aurora. "Let's go backstage to see Edward. He'll be expecting us." The girls pushed their way through the crowd, who blithely blocked exits as they stood chatting, swooping down on each other like shimmering birds and crying out in delight.

"Lady Fitzcillian! Georgiana! What a delight to see you here. How exquisite you look tonight," said a man in a voice that boomed louder than Big Ben. "Her Ladyship and I have booked a private room at the Ritz for a party to partake of a little champagne supper. Will you join us?"

"I would love to have joined you, dear Lord Cox, but I'm invited to the Café Royal with His Grace and his party."

There were more greetings going on around

them so for a moment their way was blocked again.

Rose grinned wickedly. She tossed her unruly conker-coloured curls and grabbed Aurora's hand, bowed low, kissed it and declared in her best Southwark drawl, "My dear Lady Easingford! You look so delicious in that blue crêpe de Chine I could gobble you up. Would you join us for pie and mash and a cuppa?"

Effie squawked with laughter so loudly that people turned and tutted, but although Aurora grinned, Rose could see the flush rising on her friend's creamy skin, and she wished she hadn't played the fool in public. She knew that Aurora was sensitive to her still new, and unexpected, status as the lost daughter of a lord, caught in the nether land between the world of Campion's and polite society, and feeling as if she no longer quite belonged in either.

Rory's face blushed pinker still as somebody whispered loudly, "Isn't that the Easingford girl? Aurora? Such behaviour!" Another woman, with a mouth puckered as if she had just drunk a quart of vinegar, raised her lorgnette to peer at Aurora more closely. The murmured words "dresses as a boy in a music hall act" rose like vicious little balloons from the tight gaggle of women, and there were some shocked gasps of delighted outrage. Then another whispered loudly, "They say Edward Easingford has been seen losing badly at the card tables. Maybe his daughter could support him doing her music hall turn if he runs through the Easingford fortune?"

There was malicious laughter. The women made Rose think of the geese she had spotted on the muddy banks of the Thames down by London Bridge, pecking at each other viciously if any weakness was spotted. Seeing Aurora's face, so undefended and full of hurt, Rose reached for her friend's gloved hand, squeezed it hard and pulled her through the throng with Effie following.

They reached the top of the stairs. A tall man sporting an elaborate waxed handlebar moustache and a jolly peacock-blue waistcoat, and holding a glass of brandy in his hand, was standing amid a small group of men. He was talking a little too animatedly as if trying to keep their interest. It was obvious that he was boring his companions, who one by one were slipping away. Rose felt sorry for him. She liked his bright peacock waistcoat, which looked like a gaudy costume that might be worn by an actor upon the Campion's stage, and didn't think that anyone who wore such evening clothes could possibly be dull. The waistcoat marked him out as different, and as two of the group passed, Rose heard one murmur to the other, "Interesting chap and filthy rich, of course, but in trade, and it shows. Did you see that waistcoat! Not the thing at all." She glanced back and caught the eye of the owner of the waistcoat, and his rueful smile suggested that he too had heard what had been said about him. He winked at Rose and then turned to the bar to get himself another drink.

Rose and the others leaned against the balcony and looked down past one of five chandeliers, hanging within touching distance and shimmering so brightly with coloured crystals that it made Rose think of Aladdin's treasure cave in the Campion's pantomime. The crowd below glittered too. It suddenly parted for Stratford-Mark, the portly actor-manager who owned and ran the Pall Mall, and who Rose thought resembled a mournful walrus. He acknowledged the crowd like a king. On his arm was an exquisite woman whose skin was so luminous it was as if somebody had sprinkled sugar crystals all over it, for the way it gleamed in the light. But glistening even more radiantly was the single, huge blue stone that hung around her neck on a slender gold chain. It was the colour of a dazzling sea on a summer's day. Everyone turned to look at her and the stone, and there were cries of admiration and loud whispers. Two men, looking awkward in ill-fitting evening dress, hovered nearby, looking ready to tackle anyone who came too close.

"Who is she?" breathed Rory.

"Let me enlighten you." It was the stranger in the peacock-blue waistcoat. He gave the three girls a little bow. "That is Lydia Duchamps – at least, that's what she calls herself. She arrived here in London recently, from America. Everyone says she will be a huge star. Well, Stratford-Mark does, and if he says so it must be true. He's taken a real interest in her. Nobody knows where she's come from, and the more unkind whisper that it must have been the gutter. But as Stratford-Mark has already introduced her to everyone who is anyone, the only way is up. Possibly to the very top of society. She is a shooting star, our little Miss Duchamps." The man was clearly delighted to have found a new and far more receptive audience.

"So she's an actress?" asked Rose. "Is she any good?"

"Nobody has seen her act yet. She is to make her debut as Lady Macbeth opposite Stratford-Mark himself – an unlikely coupling, I know, but they say that Stratford-Mark eventually wants to have her play opposite Edward Easingford in the great classics. Thinks they will make a pretty pair and be a huge draw together. He's got one box-office hit with *Hamlet* but he badly needs more. There are rumours that this theatre is mortgaged to the hilt, and Stratford-Mark will do anything to save it. Edward Easingford is a great actor, so does it really matter if Lydia Duchamps is not a great actress? She's certainly a great beauty, and she's got a good eye for publicity, and that's important these days."

"That gem's a real whopper," said Effie, starring at the jewel around Lydia Duchamps's neck.

"That's the famous Star of the Sea," said the man. "Those two men clinging to her like shadows are there to ensure it's not stolen." The man grinned, but without malice. "Judging by the number of swells here with secret gambling debts from too many late nights at the baccarat table, it's probably a wise precaution. Stratford-Mark isn't the only one suffering financial embarrassment. The Star is being auctioned next week – what better way to generate interest in both Lydia Duchamps and the diamond than by putting the two of them together at the most glittering first night of the season? It was a stroke of genius of Stratford-Mark to suggest it."

"A diamond?" asked Aurora. "But it's blue. I thought diamonds were white."

"Not this one," said the man. "The fact that it's blue and so flawless contributes to its value and romance, although of course some may be put off bidding because of its disturbing history."

All three girls leaned forward with curiosity. The man was enjoying their attention.

"What do you mean, disturbing history?" asked Aurora.

"The Star of the Sea is also known as the Doomstone, because so many who have owned it, or in some instances stolen it, have died in mysterious circumstances."

Effie gasped, her eyes wide.

"I think I've heard of the Doomstone," said Aurora with a frown.

"I know I have," said Rose, her eyes alight with interest. "I remember now. I read about it. They say it's cursed."

There were a large number of people swirling around outside the stage door hoping to catch a glimpse of the actors. Rose and the others managed to push their way through, and were let into the theatre by Grumbles, the ginger-whiskered stage-doorkeeper, who smelled of mothballs and had acquired his nickname because he complained unceasingly. He ushered them through, moaning about the racket outside his stage door and Stratford-Mark's parsimony, and the girls climbed the stairs. They walked along a dingy corridor, where the paint peeled from the walls – a stark contrast to front of house, all red velvet, gilt and crystal. The Pall Mall, thought Rose, was like a dowager duchess who went out dripping diamonds but underneath wore dirty petticoats. One of the dressing-room doors opened slightly and a wan girl about their own age with reddish-gold hair peered out at them. Her gooseberry-green eyes were wary, and when the ever-friendly Rose beamed at her she looked flustered and slammed the door shut again, as if Rose's smile was a threat.

Edward's dressing room was far more cheerful: full of gilt mirrors, flowers and well-dressed chattering people. Rose noticed that Edward looked simultaneously exhausted and exhilarated, and she envied him for having just come off stage having performed in one of the greatest plays ever written. She vowed to herself that one day she too would act on this stage playing the great Shakespearian heroines, Rosalind, Juliet and Viola.

Aurora had to fight her way over to her father. As soon as he saw her he grinned delightedly and hugged her hard, dropping a kiss on the top of her head. For a moment Rose felt a pang watching father and daughter together. She knew that Thomas loved her like a father, but Thomas was never demonstrative like Edward was with Rory. It was, thought Rose, as if Thomas was always conscious that he wasn't her real father, and didn't want to burden her by laying too great a claim to her. Or maybe he was protecting himself from the day that might come when someone laid claim to her, as Edward had done with Aurora just a few months ago. But Rose knew that lightning was unlikely to strike twice, even though Thomas had been doggedly pursuing the only information they had to go on about Rose's origins. All they knew was that she had been stolen as a newborn out of a pram from somewhere in the West End by the unscrupulous Lizzie Gawkin, who had dumped her like an unwanted parcel on the steps of Campion's a few days later. It was very little to go on – too little, said the police, who had been extremely unhelpful, and Rose was level-headed enough to realise that it was unlikely she would ever find her real father. Or the mother whose lack she sometimes felt so sorely. Real life wasn't like a play.

She realised that she had been lost in thought and hadn't heard what Edward was asking her.

"Rosie," said Effie, nudging her. "Ed's askin' what yer think of his performance and the production."

"You're the only person, Rose, I can really

trust to tell me the truth," said Edward, and he said it so sincerely that Rose knew that he took her opinion seriously, because he knew that acting really mattered to her. She felt a flood of happiness inside: it must mean that Edward, who was a really good actor, thought that she might be a good actor too. She began to talk earnestly to him about the production and the bits that she thought really worked, and why she didn't think the final sword fight was as successful, and how it could be better if the blocking was done differently.

Edward was nodding his agreement when the door of the dressing room opened again. Lydia Duchamps stood framed in the doorway as if she was an exquisite real-life painting, the Doomstone winking like a blue, unblinking eye at her beautiful neck. Edward stared at her for a moment as if mesmerised. Stratford-Mark lumbered forward to make the introduction, putting a proprietorial hand on her arm, as if she was a precious jewel he had recently purchased and wanted to keep safe.

"Edward, my dear boy, this is Miss Lydia—"

But before he could finish, Lydia had swept across the room to Edward, closely followed by her human shadows, and cried, "Edward, Lord Easingford, you were quite magnificent!" Her voice was low and husky, with just the tiniest trace of an American accent. "You are the talk of the town. I cannot wait to play opposite you. I will be Juliet to your Romeo, Titania to your Oberon. Together we will take London by storm."

Rose suppressed a snort of laughter, although she had to admit that being in a room with Lydia was like being in the presence of a small, exquisitely formed hurricane. Rose thought that Lydia was all too obviously putting on an act, but Effie was staring at Lydia longingly, Aurora looked impressed and none of the men and women in the room could drag their eyes away from her, including Edward. Edward bowed low and kissed Lydia's hand.

"Miss Duchamps, I am enchanted to meet you." He raised his gaze to meet hers, and as their eyes locked a tiny frisson of shock and surprise crossed Lydia's face, as if she had just been hit by a bolt of lightning that had fallen not from the sky but from Edward's eyes. For a second she swayed, and Rose wondered if she was about to faint.

"Please, call me Lydia," she said, and her voice faltered charmingly.

"I would be delighted," said Edward softly.

For a second the two of them stared at each other as if they were quite alone in the room. Stratford-Mark, watching this little scene, gave a cough, and with a struggle Lydia seemed to recover herself, and she clapped her hands girlishly.

"Now, we must all celebrate Edward's London debut." She turned to everyone. "We will hit the town and drink champagne. Shall we start at the Ritz?" There were murmurs of agreement from many in the room.

"But, Edward," said Aurora, looking worried. "I thought we were going back to Campion's to see the Illustrious Gandini do his show. That's what we agreed." Rose and Effie nodded their heads vigorously in support. It had been arranged as soon as it had been confirmed that Gandini would be performing at Campion's tonight. Edward had already invited the cast, backstage crew and Stratford-Mark, who had expressed his delight at the prospect of seeing the wizard perform. Lydia was examining Rory.

"Oh, Edward, this must be your long-lost

daughter, Aurora. The town talks of nothing but how the two of you were so romantically reunited. You look so alike. She is as pretty as a plum. A real little lady."

Aurora blushed, and Rose smiled to herself, thinking that if Lydia had seen Aurora just a few hours earlier, when she, Rose and Effie had been covered with grease and dust working backstage at Campion's, she wouldn't have recognised her. Lydia looked at Rose and Effie.

"What is this Campion's, and who is this Illustrious Gandini?"

"It's a small music hall in Southwark across the river where Effie and I live. Rory and Edward sometimes stay too when they aren't at Edward's house in Silver Square, and tonight the magician Gandini is performing there," said Rose. Then she added firmly, "We promised Thomas that we would come back after the show. He'll be expecting…" She trailed off. She could see Edward's face obviously torn between his loyalty to Campion's and the bewitching Lydia Duchamps.

Rose instinctively understood that Lydia was the sort of woman who liked to be seen and admired by the rich and powerful. For her, a place like Campion's, down at heel and the wrong side of the river, would be slumming it. Why would she want to go there tonight, when she could share Edward's triumph among the cream of society in the West End? Particularly when she was supposed to be showing off the Star of the Sea and creating interest in the upcoming auction. Nobody who lived in Southwark was going to buy it.

But to Rose's surprise, with a smile as sweet as fresh milk, Lydia said, "A promise is a promise and must not be broken. We will go to this Campion's and see if this great wizard is as great as he claims. It will be charming, I am quite sure, and we will make this little music hall the most fashionable place in London simply by being there." She tucked her arm firmly in Edward's and walked towards the door, despite the protests from the men charged with protecting the Doomstone from thieving hands. They were disconcerted by the prospect of going south of the river to an area that was notorious for its priggers and blaggers. But Lydia simply laughed at their concerns.

"I will be completely surrounded by people at a music hall. It will be impossible for the Star of the Sea to be stolen in front of everyone, with you sharp-eyed gentlemen watching my every move and with hundreds of other people present. It is probably the safest place in London tonight." She turned to Edward. "Besides, I will have his Lordship by my side. Edward will protect me from any skulduggery."

3

It took what seemed like forever to Rose to get everyone settled in coaches and cabs. Edward, Lydia, her two shadows and Stratford-Mark were settled in one. Rose and Rory and Effie got in another, and numerous other actors and hangers-on squashed into several more. Rose was beginning to worry that if they didn't hurry, the Illustrious Gandini would have finished his act. They finally appeared to be ready to move when a girl wearing a mustard-yellow dress ran out of the stage door waving her arms.

"Miss Duchamps! Miss Duchamps! Have you forgotten all about me? You told me to wait in your dressing room. You said you would return after the performance and tell me if you needed me again."

Rose recognised her as the red-haired girl they had seen peering from behind the door in the corridor. She was even lankier than Effie, and there was something of the foal about her, as if her legs were too long for her body, lending her a graceless but endearing quality. Lydia leaned out of the carriage window and put a hand to her head in a theatrical gesture.

"I'm so forgetful. Forgive me, Amy," she said with a tinkling laugh. Then she called out to everyone, as if an explanation was necessary. "Dear little Amy is my dresser while I'm at the Pall Mall. I have no further need of you tonight. You can return to your lodgings, Amy." Then, as an afterthought, she asked, "Where do you lodge, Amy?"

"Rotherhithe way, Miss Duchamps," muttered the girl, twisting her hands awkwardly and keeping her head bent.

"How convenient," said Lydia. "We will be able to give you a ride. Pop in the cab at the back. There's a spare seat. You can come with us to Campion's music hall if you so wish. That will be a treat for you, Amy."

The girl kept her eyes on the ground. "I don't know, Miss Duchamps. I don't want to impose."

"Oh, the more the merrier, I always say, although of course if you are too tired…"

"No, Miss Duchamps. Thank you, Miss Duchamps," said the girl. "I'll come to see the Illustrious Gandini." And she gave a bob and ran back to the final cab, clambering in and almost falling over her own limbs in the scramble.

"Let's go," said Lydia, clapping her hands, and the coachman snapped his whip and the party set off.

"Crikey," said Effie as their cab began to move. "That poor Amy could have bin all night at the theatre waiting for Lydia to come back, if she ain't come looking for her. Was a good thing we didn't set off a minute earlier."

"It was kind of Lydia to invite her, wasn't it?" said Aurora. "She's so glamorous and beautiful and sure of herself, I thought she might be spoilt and used to getting everything she wanted." Rose wondered whether Aurora was really trying to say that she had been worried by the way that Lydia had so obviously fixed her cap at Edward. "But I was wrong," continued Aurora. "You can see by the way she insisted that she would come along with us to Campion's when we mentioned our plans, and saw how important it was to us, that she's got a caring heart."

Rose made a non-committal noise. She thought that Lydia would have gone wherever Edward was going, even if he had announced that he planned to pop to the very ends of the earth and back. She ran over the exchange between Lydia and Amy in her head and frowned – there was something else about the conversation, something that had been said that had jarred, but she couldn't put her finger on it.

"What's wrong, Rosie?" asked Effie. "You're not worried that the curse of the Doomstone will catch up with Lydia and she'll drop down dead at Campion's in the middle of Gandini's act?"

Rose grinned. "I'm more worried those thieving Tanner Street boys will filch it while she's not looking."

"Them Tanner Street boys'll know the Doomstone's way out of their league. Ain't no fence in London will touch swag like that gem. Way too hot. Every Blue in town would be looking for it. Anyways, they wouldn't dare finger it if they knew about the curse. Them Tanner Street boys may look tough, but they're scaredy-cats. Remember how long they stayed away from Campion's when that rumour went round that you'd seen Ned Dorset's ghost, Rosie," said Effie.

Rose said nothing. She knew that she *had* seen poor, murdered Ned Dorset's ghost.

"Come on, Rosie," said Aurora. "Tell us more about the curse, and how you know about it."

"I read about the Doomstone in a copy of one of Thomas's gazettes. It said that it was looted from a palace in India in the fourteenth century. The stone was pulled from the crown of an empress whose husband had been stabbed to death by marauding invaders. Legend has it that the empress begged the soldiers to take the diamond, but to spare her twin daughters, who she was cradling in her arms. But they bayoneted the babes to death and stabbed the empress too. With her dying breath she cursed the diamond, saying that it would only ever bring grief and disaster to those who stole or owned it."

"And has it?" asked Effie, wide-eyed.

Rose nodded. "It didn't bring much luck to Marie Antoinette. She owned it and she lost her head to the guillotine during the French Revolution. Over the last century the Doomstone has turned up all over Europe, even in America, sometimes stolen and sometimes traded, and often bringing sudden death, suicide, debt and destruction in its wake. It's been in a vault for the last twelve years since the Doomstone's last owner jumped to his death after his entire family were killed in a carriage accident, and it was sold to pay off his debts."

Effie's eyes widened further. "So the curse is true! We must warn Lydia."

Rose laughed. "It's probably just a series of unfortunate coincidences. Anyway, I don't think Lydia has much to worry about. It's not as if she's stolen the diamond or owns it. After tonight she's going to give it back, and it will be auctioned next week."

"Well, I ain't buying it," said Effie, "and I don't know who would."

Rose smiled. Effie didn't have more than a tuppence to her name, and a deuce wasn't going to buy her the Doomstone.

"Rich speculators," said Rose. "They won't care about the curse as long as the price of the diamond keeps rising, and as it's the most flawless blue diamond in the world, it almost certainly will. In fact, the curse probably only adds to the fascination of the Doomstone and increases its worth."

"We've arrived," said Aurora excitedly, and she stood up before the cab had come to a halt, falling in a heap on top of Rose and Effie when it pulled up sharply.

4

They were still laughing as they piled out of the cab into Hangman's Alley, lifting their skirts as they stepped over the muddy pockmarks in the road and shooing away the yapping stray dogs. They were immediately surrounded by a throng of ragged children, their faces haunted by the exhaustion of long days in the factory or begging on the street. The girls gave them all the pennies they had.

Music spilled out on to the street from Campion's; from the roar of the crowd it was clear that a cancan led by Lottie and the ballet dancers was in full swing. Rose thought that there was no lovelier sight in the world than the golden light and the flitting shadows glimpsed through the windows of Campion's on a late summer's night. Every time the door opened the sound of merriment filtered out on to the street.

Rose glanced through the open gate into the yard that led backstage. She could just see O'Leary's feet poking out from the open stage door, where he was sitting, supposedly charged with keeping strangers out but all too often slumped in a semi-drunken stupor. Tiny Titch, a comic and singer – so-called because he was a huge giant of a man, over six feet tall and seemingly almost as wide – was chatting to Dolores, known as Queen of the Slack Wire, and Belle Canterbury, a Campion's regular whose crystal voice was so unworldly that when she sang audiences felt as if someone was running a finger down their spines. Rose was glad to see Belle back at Campion's; it must mean that her mother, to whom Belle was devoted, had recovered from her most recent illness.

Tobias Fraggles, the newish flyman, who shifted the scenery backstage, was standing smoking by the gate, gazing longingly after Lydia, who was just disappearing through the entrance to Campion's. Rose smiled to herself. Clearly Edward wasn't Lydia's only conquest tonight. The young flyman looked dazzled.

Rose glimpsed Jem Dorries, a Campion's fixture who played romantic leads in the melodramas, did a bit of magic, sang when required in his pleasing tight tenor and helped out backstage when needed. He was standing in the corner of the yard close to the gate, passing a handful of coins to a small boy. Rose guessed that Jem was using the child as a runner to place a bet, probably at this time of night on some illegal activity such as cockfighting. Jem would bet on anything. Only yesterday he had tried to get Rose to wager sixpence against him on which one of two raindrops running down a Campion's dressing-room window would reach the bottom first. She'd noted the desperation in his eyes when she refused, and hadn't been at all surprised when he had asked her if she could lend him a shilling, which she couldn't. It was always the same with Jem Dorries – he was either flush with cash or penniless. Clearly he must have had some serious luck since yesterday, when he hadn't a penny to his name.

The crowd at the box office began to move forward, but not before Rose spotted Billy Proctor, the new barman who had been taken on a couple of days back, just after Gandini's appearance had been announced. He was on his own smoking moodily in the shadows of the yard. Thomas had said they were short-handed, and with the extra custom that Gandini would bring in, it was an ideal time to hire a new member of staff. Rose hadn't taken to Billy Proctor. He was surly, as if he thought being a barman was beneath him, and he was slow and clumsy when serving, and kept popping up unexpectedly in places backstage where he had no business being. What was he doing in the yard at this time of an evening when Campion's was packed? Just before setting out for the Pall Mall this evening, she had seen him outside Gandini's dressing room. The door was ajar and he'd appeared to be eavesdropping on Gandini and Jem, who were playing cards together.

When he realised Rose had spotted him, Billy had scuttled away, something shifty in his manner. Rose had lingered for a moment to see if Billy returned, and Gandini, suddenly aware of her presence through the gap in the door, had courteously bowed his head at Rose in such a gentlemanly manner she had almost wanted to curtsy. Thinking about it, Rose wondered whether Jem had taken money off Gandini at cards, and that's where his money had come from. If he had beaten Gandini at cards, it was hardly the greatest advertisement for the Great Wizard's supposed skills.

Edward, Lydia and Stratford-Mark were already inside by the time Rose and the others passed under the legend that declared "Campion's Palace of Varieties and Wonders." They walked through the new double-fronted door, flanked with intricate plasterwork decorated with fruits and vines, painted in fresco colours and picked out in gold leaf. They were immediately enveloped in the welcoming, warm fug of Campion's. Rose thought it was like no other smell in the world: it was the cosy smell of home. There was a clamour of people talking, a piano tinkling and the faint hiss of the gaslights. Rose realised that Amy was standing right next to her, looking as nervous as a newborn foal and scowling slightly as she looked around. Rose tried to set the girl at ease. She was clearly highly strung.

"Have you seen Gandini perform before?" she asked, trying to make conversation. Amy seemed startled by her question.

"No," she mumbled. "Of course not. I'd never even heard of him until Miss Duchamps told me to come with everyone here tonight." Amy had dark shadows under her eyes. Maybe the poor girl was just exhausted and would have preferred to have gone home to sleep, rather than being dragged to Campion's.

With a wide beam, Thomas beckoned them towards a large vacant table in the centre of the room that he had saved for their return. It was just as well, because Campion's was crammed like an overfilled meat pie. Several small, sooty boys were clinging like monkeys to the gilt candy-cane pillars that looked far too slender to support the horseshoe balcony. It seemed that the whole of Southwark, and most of Bermondsey too, wanted to see the Illustrious Gandini perform his magic act.

But the crowd parted as best they could, and all eyes turned away from the stage, where Campion's regular Molly, who did acrobatic tricks hanging by her teeth from a strap above the stage, was performing. Eyes swivelled to watch Edward and Lydia as the pair moved slowly through the room to the vacant table. The diamond around Lydia's neck caught the light and something seemed to glow and move in its depths, just as an ocean shifts and changes. Edward had become a familiar figure around Campion's, even taking to the stage occasionally to play a small part in one of the melodramas, which had endeared him to the Campion's crowd. They knew he had a title but they afforded him no special treatment, and were as likely to boo him as anyone else if he bored them. Toff or no toff, the Campion's audience never stood on ceremony – when they handed over their hard-earned money they expected to be royally entertained, and they didn't care if it was a lord on stage or a pauper. They were fascinated to see him looking so handsome in full evening dress, with the beautiful, luminous Lydia on his arm. There were a number of whistles and saucy shouts as they progressed across the room.

"I hear you triumphed, my boy," said Thomas above the hubbub as the two men hugged each other warmly. Thomas was only a decade older than Edward, but he had swiftly become something of a father figure to the younger man.

Edward introduced Thomas to Lydia, who gave Thomas her hand and a look as soft as butter, before sinking gracefully into one of the seats.

"That bauble weighing you down, luv?" called somebody loudly from the gallery, much to the delight of the crowd, who hooted and whistled.

"Bring it 'ere, ducks. If it's too 'eavy for yer, I'll look after it," shouted another.

Effie plucked at Thomas's sleeve. "Any news from Holloway Prison about my ma?"

"I'm sorry, Effie. No," said Thomas gently. "As soon as I hear any further news I will let you know at once."

Rose noticed that a vein in Thomas's neck was twitching, a sure sign that he was anxious. "Is everything all right?" she whispered.

Thomas splashed her a smile. "You don't miss a thing, Rose Campion," he said with a hint of pride in his voice. "You're as sharp as a tiger's tooth." He lowered his voice. "I was backstage just before you arrived, and Gandini looked terrible. Very pale. Beads of sweat on his brow. As if he had a bad fever. Said he was fine, that he'd eaten a dodgy oyster and it would pass. I hope it does and he's able to perform, because otherwise we're going to have to give this lot their money back. They're up for a good night out, and if Gandini is a no-show they'll be sure to make their displeasure very clear."

Rose pulled a face, remembering the night there had been a near riot at Campion's, when the audience had taken against Aurora when she was still performing as the Infant Phenomenon.

Molly left the stage and the band struck up. There was a clash of cymbals. The Illustrious Gandini was about to appear. The crowd quietened and leaned forward, ready to enjoy themselves. Rose glanced around. She was surprised to see the man with the peacock waistcoat and handlebar moustache who had told them about the Doomstone leaning casually against the bar, and even more surprised to see that he and Billy Proctor were deep in conversation. He couldn't have known who she and the others were when he chatted to them at the theatre, and he hadn't been one of their party, so it was an odd coincidence that he had ended up at Campion's too. He saw her looking his way and tipped his top hat at her with another friendly wink, as if his being there was the most natural thing in the world.

The two men assigned to protect the Star of the Sea moved closer behind Lydia, so that she was hemmed in from the rear. Edward was sitting on one side of her and Thomas took a chair to the other side. Rory sat beside her father, and Effie was perched on Rose's knee next to Thomas. Stratford-Mark was also sitting at the table, drumming his fingers as if impatient. Rose couldn't help thinking that outside of his own domain, the Pall Mall, he seemed a little diminished. Amy had somehow wriggled her way between the two guards, so she was standing as close as possible to Lydia, like a third little shadow. She kept glancing around nervously, as if fearing an imminent attack on her employer and ready to repel it.

Many of the rest of the party who had come from the Pall Mall were at the bar. But a number of Campion's regulars had crowded around their table too. Jem was there with Belle Canterbury, as were Lottie and Tessa and several other ballet dancers, and Tobias Fraggles had found himself a spot close to Lydia. It was so cramped that everyone was pressing up against everyone else to try and get a better view. Billy Proctor squeezed his way through the throng with a tray and delivered champagne, hot brandy toddies, lemonade and platters of oysters, sprats, kidneys and poached eggs to the table. Ophelia the cat, who had been sitting on the edge of the stage, jumped down and padded through the hall, settling under the table and rubbing herself against Rose's legs. Rose reached over for a sprat and dropped it under the table for the cat. Ophelia purred her thanks.

The gaslights suddenly fluttered. There was a flash of flame, which made many in the audience scream, and Thomas half rose to his feet – any naked flame on the stage area with the lights was an accident waiting to happen. But before he could fully stand up the flame died, there was a big puff of smoke and, as if he had suddenly materialised from nowhere, the Illustrious Gandini could be glimpsed on stage wreathed in plumes of smoke. He walked forward. The audience clapped and cheered wildly as they examined the Great Wizard of the North with interest. He was a tall, thin man with exceptionally long, lanky legs and a thick black beard and moustache. His green eyes glittered in a pale face that couldn't be described as handsome but which drew the eye. He wore evening dress under a crimson cape covered in tiny silver stars, and on his dark head was a small bejewelled ruby-red fez. The overall effect was mysterious and exotic. Rose and Thomas leaned forward. Was the illustrious Gandini going to be worth his hefty fee?

Gandini bowed to the audience, and with a knowing smile reached into his pocket and produced a shiny shilling. Rose noticed that his hands were shaking slightly. There was a sheen of sweat on his top lip. He raised the shilling up into the air so that everyone could see it. Then, rotating it so that it caught the light, he placed it very deliberately in the open palm of his raised left hand. One by one his fingers closed over the coin and it gradually disappeared from view until all the audience could see was his raised clenched fist. Then with a flourish he passed his right hand in a quick circular motion over his fisted hand as if performing a spell, and opened the palm of his left hand wide. It was completely empty.

There was gasp from the crowd, followed by wild applause. But the Illustrious Gandini put a finger to his lips to quieten them. He walked down the steps in front of the stage and, pushing past the tables at the front – including one where three men were drinking brandy – he made his way over to the table next to Rose and the others.

"Excuse me, sir," he said to an elderly man, and he reached behind the man's ear and pulled out a shiny shilling. The audience laughed. The Illustrious Gandini flipped the coin in the air and then handed it to the man. Gandini's eyes sparkled like a shifting sage-grey sea.

"Keep it, sir; a memento for you and your lovely wife of your evening together." He bowed low to the elderly man's companion, and the audience warmed to his gentlemanly air. Then he turned and started walking back towards the stage. But as he reached the table closest to the stage where the three portly, red-faced men were sitting, he swivelled back to the audience and then asked the men, "Have any of you gentlemen mislaid anything?"

"No," said one of the men. But then he patted his waistcoat. "My watch! My watch is missing!"

"So's mine!" said both the other men simultaneously, a note of concern in their voices.

"No need to panic, gentlemen," said Gandini, and he pulled all three of their watches from the depths of his cape and laid them on the table. "The Illustrious Gandini does not steal, he merely borrows."

The men clapped wildly and so did the rest of the audience. Gandini seemed in complete control. The colour bloomed in his cheeks again. His hands were steady. The magician took a bow, shook hands with each of the gentlemen, clapped them each on the shoulder and turned to mount the stairs back on to the stage. But then he spun round again.

"Gentlemen," he said, a twinkle in his eye, "I fear that all three of you are ridiculously careless with your timepieces."

Once again the men registered their loss as Gandini pulled the three watches from his cape once more, and the audience dissolved with laughter at the trio's blustering bewilderment.

"They're plants: friends of the wizard. There's no magic here," shouted a pockmarked youth with a livid scar on his cheek, who was standing at the edge of the auditorium, slouching against the wall. Rose turned. It was one of the Tanner Street boys. They were always trouble. Gandini smiled lazily and sauntered over to him. Rose held her breath. You didn't mess with any of the Tanner Street boys.

"You do not believe in my magic?" he asked the youth politely.

43

"Nah, it's all a set-up; you're just tricking us," said the young man, an aggressive, drunken edge in his voice.

"Sir is free to believe what he wishes. If he has seen with his own eyes and still doesn't believe, I will happily refund your price of admission," replied Gandini very calmly.

"Yeah, why don't you do that? I've seen enough. It's rubbish." There were some boos from the audience; they didn't think it was rubbish.

"I'll get my money," said Gandini, and he turned back towards the stage. But he had taken just a few steps when the youth, infuriated by Gandini's unruffled politeness and the boos from the crowd, lurched after him. The lad had only taken a stride or two when his trousers slipped down around his ankles. As the audience realised what had happened they began to break out in gales of mocking laughter. Nobody liked the Tanner Street boys. Even their mum had been heard to observe that they were a menace.

"Oh dear," said Gandini, holding up the young man's belt. "You seem to have been very careless and lost your trouser belt." The audience screamed with delighted laughter. For a second it seemed as if the Tanner Street boy was going to punch Gandini, but as if reading his mind, the Wizard of the North clapped him on the shoulder and said, "A free tankard of porter for my young friend, please, for being such a good sport."

Rose caught Thomas's eye. They both knew that Gandini was simply using sleight of hand to bamboozle the audience with his tricks, but it was the way he was mentally manipulating them that was so fascinating. Learning to be a first-rate magician took years of hard work, but Gandini had appeared to spring from nowhere. There had been no years of working his way up the bill on the northern music-hall circuit and refining his act performance by performance for him. He had just appeared with a flourish, like a puff of magic itself, and was immediately in demand. He cultivated the air of a man of mystery. It made Rose wonder what he was doing here at Campion's, when he could have his pick of any hall, including much larger places where the fees would be a dozen times what Thomas could ever offer.

Gandini was now in the middle of a card trick,

in which a young woman who he had led from her seat in the audience up on to the stage had randomly selected and marked a card, the queen of diamonds, without Gandini – who had been blindfolded – seeing it. She had then returned it to the pack. Gandini, still blindfolded, was now shuffling the pack energetically. Then with a flourish he took the very top card from the pack and held it up. It was the woman's marked queen of diamonds. There was loud applause as Gandini removed his blindfold. The audience were completely gripped. They could not take their eyes off Gandini, watching his every move and trying to work out how he was fooling them. Even those right at the back of the hall by the bar had fallen silent. Several had weaved their way forward through the crowd. Rose noticed that the man with the handlebar moustache from the Pall Mall was now hard up by their table, just behind the men guarding the Doomstone. The Tanner Street boy was there too, his temper recovered by a free drink. Gandini kissed the hand of the woman from the audience and encouraged the crowd to give her a round of applause as he led her back to her seat. As she went to sit down, she gave a little gasp. There on her chair was the queen of diamonds that she had marked! She held it up to the audience and there was a buzz of astonishment before more enthusiastic applause.

Gandini bowed again, just as Billy Proctor arrived at Rose's table with more champagne and extra glasses. Gandini had gone to stand behind a small table situated on the left-hand side of the stage. The table was covered in a dark-green velvet cloth. Gandini removed the cloth and held up the table, twirling it in the air and demonstrating to the audience that it had no hidden compartments. He put down the table and covered it again with the velvet tablecloth, and then he took off his red, jewelled fez, showed the empty interior to the audience and placed it upside down on the table. The gaslights hissed and flickered. There was a puff of smoke that seemed to come from inside the fez, and then the sound of fluttering wings. Suddenly a dove flew out of it, followed by another, and another.

"Everyone count the doves!" commanded Gandini. The audience gasped and squealed and their eyes grew as round as saucers as bird after bird emerged from the tiny fez and flew in a circle around the Illustrious Gandini's head.

The audience started counting out loud.

"One … two … three…" They couldn't believe what they were seeing as more than a dozen white doves flew out of the small red hat and just kept coming. It was impossible! The audience went crazy, laughing and shouting out their pleasure.

A woman's piercing scream cut across the clamour. Lydia rose to her feet, pushing her chair away and forcing the crush of people around the table to step backwards. She was pale and shaking, and she had her hand to her white neck. Small droplets of ruby blood were clearly visible on her neck and smeared across her hand. She clawed at her neck, her eyes full of terror and shouted, "Somebody has tried to kill me. The Doomstone! The Doomstone has been stolen!" Then she fainted dead away, and would have fallen to the floor if Edward had not caught her.

For a split second it was clear that some people thought this might be all part of the show. But the blood was definitely real, and Gandini looked shocked and bewildered. Amy screamed and then began to whimper. The cry of "Murder!" went up from several corners of the hall. Mayhem erupted all around Campion's. The two men who had been guarding the Star of the Sea looked wildly around and started yelling for the coppers. Thomas called for a doctor, and a man stepped forward to help. The audience were on their feet, pointing at Lydia and shouting.

"Somebody cut 'er throat to prig that gem!"

"It's the curse, the curse of the Doomstone!" shouted Effie, her eyes wide with fright.

Amy looked terrified out of her wits, as if wishing that she was anywhere else but Campion's. Gandini seemed simultaneously frightened and angry. Billy Proctor had a frown on his face. Stratford-Mark was sweating profusely, and looked both excited and terrified. Edward had wrapped his white silk evening scarf around Lydia's slender neck to stem the blood and was fanning her face. The doctor who had come forward kneeled down beside Lydia. Her eyes fluttered and she moaned quietly. Thomas strode up on to the stage and raised his hands to quieten the crowd.

"I'm afraid that the show cannot go on tonight. There has been a serious accident. I'm sorry but everyone must leave immediately."

Some people were already making their way to the door – they didn't want to be around when the Blues arrived. Others were shuffling closer to have a good gawp at Lydia. This was so much better than any show.

"Mr Campion is right, people should leave. But not quite everyone," said a commanding voice, and a man of about fifty with dark sideburns and a pleasant, open face moved up on to the stage. "I am Inspector Cliff of Scotland Yard. Most of you can go, but I would like to talk to anyone who thinks they saw the attack on Miss Duchamps. I shall also need to speak to everyone sitting at the same table as Miss Duchamps, Lord Easingford and Mr Campion, and all those crowded around it." He pointed at the Tanner Street boy who was trying to creep towards the door.

"And that definitely includes you, young man." He nodded to a policeman who had just arrived, who took the protesting Tanner Street boy's arm. The inspector turned to the two bodyguards, who looked stunned as if they couldn't believe that the diamond really had been stolen.

"I'll want to interview you both immediately."

He turned to Gandini. "I will need to talk to you too, sir."

The magician nodded. He looked genuinely shaken. "Is she all right?" he kept asking anxiously. "She's not dead?" Stratford-Mark was asking the same question urgently. The inspector shook his head.

Rose glanced around. Amy was snivelling quietly. Billy Proctor was back at the bar, wiping glasses and looking entirely unconcerned. Lottie, Jem and the others were all whispering to each other. There was somebody missing: the man in the peacock waistcoat who had spoken to them at the Pall Mall and told them about the Star of the Sea was nowhere to be seen. He must have slipped away. Rose frowned. He had been standing very close to Lydia, and the inspector had asked everyone crowding around the table to stay, so why leave – unless he had a reason why he didn't want to be interviewed by the police? In fact, why had he come to Campion's at all? He hadn't introduced himself when he started talking to them, and they had all been so fascinated by what he had to tell them about the diamond that Rose hadn't noticed, but now she wondered who he really was and whether his presence at Campion's tonight was just a coincidence.

"I assume that you can make a room available for me, Mr Campion," said Inspector Cliff, "so that I can start my investigation into the attempted murder of Miss Lydia Duchamps and the theft of the Star of the Sea."

5

Rose, Aurora and Effie were downstairs in the Campion's auditorium. It was mid-morning and all three of them were yawning because they had got to bed so late. Campion's was still full of policemen who were searching the place from top to bottom for a second time, looking for the missing diamond. The previous night, straight after the show, the police had taken apart the auditorium and the stage, Thomas's study and Gandini's dressing room. The magician hadn't seemed in the least bit offended by the attention, even when the inspector had asked to do a body search – a request he had made of all the men present. Gandini had merely raised an eyebrow and said with an amused smile, "Come now, Inspector, you must know that I'm not really a magician. I was never anywhere near Miss Duchamps. I would have to be able to do real magic to have flown over to Miss Duchamps's table, slit her throat and stolen the Doomstone while all the time appearing to be standing on the stage with doves flying around my head."

The inspector nodded and looked uncomfortable, but replied pleasantly, "I know it's all smoke and mirrors, sir, but I can exclude nobody from my investigation at this stage."

Gandini had smiled easily. "I will help you in every way I can, Inspector. I have nothing to hide and I don't like seeing a beautiful woman nearly getting her throat cut. It offends me."

The girls had a copy of *The Times* spread out on the table in front of them. Rose had already read aloud the ecstatic review of Edward's Hamlet to the others, not just once, but three times. She had just finished reading out a long report on what had happened last night at Campion's for the second time.

Effie's eyes were wide. "Read that bit again, Rosie, 'bout the doves and Lydia screaming an' clutching her neck with bloodied hands as if a vampire had sunk his fangs into her throat."

Rose laughed. "I don't think there's a single

word about vampires in the report, Effie. You've made that up. If you'd just let me try to teach you to read and write you could read the story yourself, and as many novels and stories about vampires as you wanted."

Effie loved stories but she couldn't read or write properly. She said that when she looked at a page all the letters seemed to be dancing around as if on purpose to confuse her. She was embarrassed by her lack of skill, and only Rose, Aurora and Thomas knew the true extent of her difficulty, even though Rose had pointed out that probably at least half of those working at Campion's found reading and writing a challenge. But Effie would not be comforted about her failure to read and write.

"I know that, Rosie, but most of 'em never went to school. I did until I was eleven and I still can't read and write proper." She sighed. "It must be because I'm stupid. That's what they said I was at school."

But Rose, Aurora and Thomas knew that Effie was far from stupid. She was remarkable with her fingers and could work out how to fix equipment that sometimes even the stagehands said was broken beyond repair. Only last week she had managed to repair part of the trap that Tobias Fraggles had insisted needed to be replaced, which had clearly narked the flyman, who muttered mutinously about "girls being let loose" in the workshop. He had complained to Thomas, who had given him short shrift. Thomas knew Effie's worth. She could draw exceptionally well too, catching a likeness of anyone. And she also had an extraordinary imagination, and was always making up stories, the bloodier and more ghoulish the better. She liked to tell them to Rose and Aurora as the three of them lay in bed together late at night. Although recently, Aurora and Edward had been spending more time at the Easingford London residence, an imposing house in Silver Square, so it had only been Effie and Rose top to tail in the bed, which wasn't quite the same. They were a trio.

"All right, I'll read it one more time," said Rose, seeing Effie's pleading face.

"It's so detailed," said Aurora. "Almost as if the reporter was actually there."

"He'd have asked around," said Effie. "There were loads of people there. All them swells from up West. And half of Southwark and

Bermondsey were out for the night. An' they all hung around long after the hall was cleared. Bet they were all ready to tell everything what they saw to any reporter prepared to dish 'em a penny or two."

Rose frowned. "But that's the odd thing, isn't it? There were three hundred or more witnesses to the crime and it seems not a single one of us actually saw anything happen, even though the lights were up and Lydia was sitting in full view of everyone."

"That's because we were all lookin' at them doves," said Effie sagely. "We didn't have eyes for anything else."

"Well," said Rose, "somebody stole the Star of the Sea, so who do you two think did it?"

There was a small cough, and they looked up guiltily to see Lydia leaning against one of the gilt pillars, looking as fragile and delicate as a priceless porcelain vase. She was pale as morning milk. A bandage was wrapped around her neck.

"Lydia! Miss Duchamps!" exclaimed Aurora, jumping up and offering her chair. "Should you be up? Are you feeling better?"

Lydia smiled wanly as she sat down. Thomas

had found her a bed at Campion's, after the doctor had suggested that she was in a shocked state and should not be moved.

"I still feel a little dizzy," she whispered, and her fingers wandered to her neck. Tears welled in her eyes. "I've had a lucky escape. I could have been murdered." She looked fearfully around. "I should never have agreed to wear the Doomstone. But I didn't see how one night could matter. I thought the story of the curse was a foolish tale, but I was the fool not to heed it. I almost lost my life to the curse." She shivered. "It may yet catch up with me."

Effie was nodding sympathetically. Aurora took Lydia's hand and patted it soothingly. Rose gave a quick supportive smile, but she thought that Lydia was being over-dramatic. She had heard the doctor tell Thomas and the inspector that the wounds to Lydia's neck were superficial. Lydia glanced curiously at the open copy of *The Times*.

"Has the newspaper reported the theft of the diamond?" she asked. "Does it give the whole story?"

"Yes," said Effie. "We've all just bin reading it. It's very exciting. Specially the bit where you almost get your throat cut."

"Lydia, has the inspector questioned you yet?" asked Aurora.

Lydia nodded. "Yes, he asked me lots of questions." She sighed. "But I'm afraid I was of very little help to him, although he was very kind. I was the victim of a terrible crime. I might have been killed. But, as I told him, I do not remember anything. Maybe it was the shock. I felt nothing until I realised there was blood on my neck. Surely those two men standing so close behind me must have seen something? One minute the diamond was there, and the next it was not, and I was bleeding. It is a great mystery. I wonder whether those two men were not quite what they seemed."

"I'm sure the inspector will have thought of that," said Rose.

"I'm sure he has. Is Edward here?" she asked Aurora, who shook her head.

"He's gone to the house at Silver Square to bathe and change. *The Times* is doing an interview with him at the Pall Mall this afternoon."

"How thrilling," said Lydia, but she looked disappointed. "I must go soon myself." Then she asked, "And what has happened to the Great Wizard of the North?"

"Gone to his lodgings," said Effie. "Them coppers were questioning him for ages, but I reckon they lost interest in him. They turned his dressing room upside down and they didn't find a blinking thing. They even looked in his fez and they didn't find no stolen diamond, not even a dove."

"It's impossible for Gandini to have stolen the Doomstone," said Rose thoughtfully. "He didn't come anywhere near our table, and he would have had to have done that to steal the diamond. When he was doing his act, I notice he'd always been close at some point to the person he's bamboozling, and he didn't come near our table."

Lydia gazed levelly at her. "You are very observant, Rose," she said.

Rose was still frowning. "There's something else. I hadn't thought of this before. But isn't it a coincidence that one of Scotland Yard's leading detectives was in the audience here on the very night that the Doomstone was stolen?"

Aurora hooted with laughter. "You aren't suggesting that the detective is the culprit, are you, Rose? That would be just too unlikely. That kind of thing only ever happens in plays."

"I wasn't suspecting the inspector of stealing the Doomstone," said Rose. "I was just wondering why he was here at all. Did he have some reason to think that something was going to happen, and the Doomstone would be stolen? Was he on the tail of somebody who he thought was a criminal?"

"Or maybe he's just a big music-hall fan? Blimey, Rosie, you do like to make things complicated," said Effie.

Lydia laughed. "Effie's right, Rose. The inspector can't possibly have known that the Doomstone was going to be stolen. After all, I was wearing it, and I had no idea myself that I'd be coming to Campion's last night until minutes before we set off. I had expected to be showing off the jewel in the Ritz, and then maybe later at the Alhambra or somewhere else in the West End, but I could never have known that I'd find myself in a little music hall down by the Thames. So how could the thief?"

Rose shrugged. That was true, so it must just be a coincidence that Inspector Cliff was in the audience.

Lydia suddenly gasped. "I quite forgot. Little Amy! Whatever happened to poor little Amy?"

"The three of us took her in a cab over to Rotherhithe after the inspector had spoken to us all together."

"How kind of you to go out of your way," murmured Lydia.

"She was terribly shaken up," said Rose. Everyone had tried to comfort her, even Gandini, who had spoken to her in a low, calming voice.

"I feel responsible for her, although I hardly know the child. Did the inspector question her?" asked Lydia.

"Yes," said Effie. "He spoke to us all together. Just like the rest of us, Amy said she was watching them doves. She was really upset she couldn't be of more help to the inspector, wasn't she, Rosie? It was almost as if she thought the whole thing was her fault."

Rose nodded. They had barely been able to get a word out of Amy, who shook like a leaf all the way to Rotherhithe, as if she was very frightened and expected her throat to be slit next. She kept trying to get them to drop her before they got to her lodgings, saying she didn't want to be any trouble. But Rose had insisted they take her right to her door, and they had watched her as she disappeared down an alley and turned into a back gate.

"Well, it seems that there are very few leads for the police," said Lydia.

"Except," said Rose, "I did tell the inspector about the man we saw. The one with the handlebar moustache and blue waistcoat who spoke to us at the Pall Mall and told us about the Doomstone. He seemed to know a great deal about its sale. Then he turned up here at Campion's too. I told the inspector that I'd seen him talking to Billy Proctor and that then he just melted away."

"Oh," said Lydia. "It could be an important lead. Clever girl, Rose. You could be the one with the crucial piece of information that solves the mystery of the stolen Doomstone. Though I say good riddance to it. No diamond, however valuable, is worth a curse on your head. I wouldn't want it anywhere near me again."

Rose hoped the inspector had taken note of what she had told him about the man. She would like to be the one to help solve the mystery.

"Well, I must go," said Lydia. "But I must say, although I was robbed and almost met my death here, Campion's really is very quaint."

Rose felt slightly insulted to hear Campion's called quaint, but she said graciously, "You must come again. You can come and see Rory and me perform our bicycle act together. Rory dresses up as a boy. It's been quite a hit."

Lydia looked scandalised. "You appear on stage dressed as a boy? Does your father approve?"

"He loves Campion's as much as we do," said Rose firmly, because she had seen the flicker of dismay that had crossed Aurora's face.

"He is so forward-thinking," trilled Lydia. "I might call by the Pall Mall and see if Edward is there. In any case, I promised Stratford-Mark I would visit today. We have my debut and other business to discuss." She saw Tobias Fraggles hanging around watching her with a look of awe on his face. She gave him a dazzling smile with just a hint of a promise in it. "Would you be a dear and find me a hansom?" she asked.

He nodded happily and raced away. Lydia left looking much brighter and far less fragile than she had a few minutes previously.

Thomas appeared almost immediately after Lydia had gone. He had confided to Rose that he was worried that the police would close Campion's down for several days, which would be terrible for business, and that when they reopened all the adverse publicity might make people stay away. But he was beaming.

"Good news, girls," he said. "The inspector says that Campion's can open tonight and carry on after all. In fact, he seems very keen to encourage business as usual."

"But will people come?" asked Rose.

Thomas grinned. "Nothing will keep them away. It seems that notoriety is good for business. Most of the tables for tonight and tomorrow have already been reserved by swells from up West." He added drily, "I don't think it's the acts so much as an opportunity to see the scene of the crime that's the main attraction. But punters are punters for whatever reason they've come." He paused dramatically with a twinkle in his eye. "And of course, when I announce that the Illustrious Gandini will be continuing to perform at Campion's for a limited engagement, they'll be beating the front door down."

"I hope not," said Rose with a grin. "That new door was very expensive." She looked thoughtful. "If Gandini is staying, it's all the more reason to think that he didn't have anything to do with the disappearance of the Doomstone."

"Yes," agreed Effie. "If he 'ad anything to hide he'd have scarpered quick."

"How long is Gandini going to perform at Campion's?" asked Aurora.

"He hasn't said," replied Thomas, "but he indicated that he intends to stay long enough to require an assistant." He looked pointedly at the trio. "I wondered whether one of you would like to volunteer?"

"It's not for me," said Aurora quickly.

Rose was surprised. She would love to be a magician's assistant, and she was certain that Aurora, who was as passionate about performing as she was, would like to be one too. "Why ever not?" blurted Rose.

A flicker of embarrassment crossed Aurora's face. "I just don't think it's quite right for me, not now, not now that…" She trailed off and looked awkwardly away from Rose as if she couldn't quite meet her eye.

Rose inwardly cursed Lydia's questioning the appropriateness of a lord's daughter performing on the Campion's stage, and she suddenly felt bereft. In the few months they had known each other she and Rory had become firm friends, a bond further strengthened by the fact that they had been abandoned together as tiny babies side by side on the front step of Campion's. Aurora had sworn that the discovery she was the daughter of a toff would make no difference to her, and when she and Edward had chosen to live in London over Easingford Hall, the family estate in Yorkshire, Rose had been thrilled. But she was beginning to realise that both she and Aurora had been naive to think that life could just go on as before. Aurora was a lady. Rose wondered whether the days of them doing the bicycle act together were numbered, and she felt a pang of sadness at the gap that had opened up between them because of an accident of birth.

"Well, if Ror don't want it, I'd love to be a magician's assistant. I'd think I'd died and gone to heaven to find meself on stage with the Illustrious Gandini. Me ma would be so proud if she could see me," said Effie.

Rose and Aurora starred at Effie in surprise. She had never been one for the limelight, always preferring to stay backstage while her two friends did their bicycle act and vied affectionately with each other to play the juvenile roles. Rose had never expected that Effie would want to do it.

Thomas glanced at her meaningfully. "Rosie? Is that all right with you if Effie tries out with Gandini?"

"Of course," said Rose brightly, determined not to show her disappointment. She smiled at Effie. "You'll be brilliant, Effie, just brilliant."

Thomas turned to Effie. "I've got more good news for you, Effie. Mr Cherryble and Edward's lawyers have secured a visit to Holloway, so you can see your mother. But it will take about a week for the paperwork to be done." Effie gave a scream of delight and flung her arms around Thomas. But Rose saw that Thomas's eyes were sad. Even with all the clout of the lawyers, Effie's mother must be very sick indeed if the prison authorities were allowing her daughter to visit her.

6

It was an early Friday night at Campion's – over a week after what the newspapers, the penny dreadfuls and the latest edition of the *Illustrated Police News* had christened "the crime of the century". There was so much newspaper interest that Thomas joked that at least half the Campion's audience was made up of journalists, all of them on expenses, which was why the bar-takings had been so staggering over the last few nights. Rose thought he may be right. Inspector Cliff certainly did. He had asked everyone at Campion's to be circumspect about talking to people he referred to as "the gentlemen of the press", because that was the way rumours were spread that might not be helpful to his investigation. Inspector Cliff clearly didn't like the journalists, and they showed little sign of liking him. There had been much baiting in the press about his failure to discover the whereabouts of the Doomstone and make an immediate arrest.

Thomas had another reason for wanting to keep anyone connected with Campion's from gossiping to the newspapermen. He feared for Campion's reputation. Earlier in the year he had faced huge debts and had almost lost Campion's. Although the immediate danger was past, the fact that he had been in financial difficulty was well known, and he knew that with the disappearance of the Doomstone, journalists would be looking to rake up any muck they could about him or Campion's. He didn't want anything to threaten Campion's future.

Rose gazed around as she helped to stack glasses. On stage, the Fabulous Flying Fongolis were more than living up to their name as they tossed each other across the stage with acrobatic flair. Campion's was packed out again, as it had been for every performance since the disappearance of the Doomstone, even though Gandini had not once topped the bill since that night.

Gandini said that he wanted to get used to working with Effie as his assistant before he performed again. He and Effie could be found together every morning, working either in his dressing room or on the Campion's stage, where onlookers were not welcomed – although that didn't stop Inspector Cliff loitering whenever he wanted.

Rose wondered whether the press might be right, and Inspector Cliff wasn't entirely on top of the investigation. She had told him about the man in the peacock waistcoat who had spoken to her and the others at the Pall Mall, and how the man had turned up at Campion's and then mysteriously disappeared. But although the inspector had made a note of what she said, she could tell that the policeman wasn't as interested as she thought he should be in what she had told him. He had seemed dismissive when she said she had seen the man talking to Billy Proctor, and that he might know his identity.

Inspector Cliff had conducted no further formal interviews or searches. He simply seemed to be hanging around Campion's a great deal, stopping to chat to people in a casual way and watching the everyday activities that went on around the music hall. That included sometimes watching Effie and Gandini try out the new act. Gandini didn't seem to mind or, if he did, he was disguising it very well.

"Ah, Inspector Cliff," he said with a smile one morning, as Rose was passing through the bar area, "soon you will know all my secrets."

"Do you have something to hide, Mr Gandini?" answered the inspector affably, and Gandini had roared with laughter.

"Ah, Inspector, you do like your little jokes."

Rose was reminded of two big cats warily circling each other, both respectful but both determined to come out on top in any fight.

The inspector wasn't the only one lurking around. She had walked upstairs that morning looking for Thomas, only to find Billy Proctor just slipping out of Thomas's study. He had looked startled to see her, which had made her suspicious, and her mistrust of him had increased when she opened the door and discovered that Thomas wasn't there. What had Billy been doing in there? Maybe Thomas had asked him to fetch something for him? She wondered whether she should tell Thomas what she'd seen, but she feared that Thomas, who always thought the best of everyone, would think her a mean-minded sneak.

Every spare minute she had, Effie was busy practising in any empty corner of Campion's she could find. Thomas said it was a good thing because it would keep her from fretting about her mother. Sometimes, when she got stuck on a basic move, Lottie, who had once filled in as a magician's assistant for a few weeks, or Jem, would try and help her.

"Lottie's almost as hopeless as me. But Jem ain't bad. He ain't a great magician, not like Gandini," said Effie sagely, "but he's bin a real help. An' he's got really good at card tricks. Says Gandini has been giving him some top tips."

Rose and Aurora had tried to get Effie to spill some secrets, but she shook her head and refused to tell them what she and Gandini were going to be performing.

"Will he saw you in half?" demanded Rose.

"Will he make you disappear?" asked Aurora.

"I'll make you two disappear if yer keep on asking me," grinned Effie and she leaned forward and produced an egg from behind Rose's ear. Aurora and Rose goggled.

"That's pure magic, Effie," said Aurora.

"Nah," said Effie, "it ain't. Fact is, more I learn from Gandini, more I think magic and prigging are pretty much the same. Them's both a deception. It's just one's for gain and other's for entertainment."

"What do you mean?" asked Rose.

"It's like this. If you're going to prig you need sharp fingers and sharp eyes. But you also need a sharp mind. When a prigger wants to filch a pocket watch, they don't just choose the first pigeon them sees walking down the street. They choose their mark carefully, someone who they think will be easier to fool. An then they distract 'im. Same with magic. Just with magic, the audience are more than up to be fooled and the magician plays on that."

"Oh, Effie," said Rory longingly. "Please, please tell us one of Gandini's secrets. Just a little one."

"All right," said Effie with a goblin smile, "but yer must cross yer hearts and promise never to tell a soul."

"We promise," chorused Rose and Rory, their eyes alight with excitement at the thought that they were at last going to discover every detail of one of Gandini's tricks.

"Well," said Effie, her face solemn, "that Gandini uses hair dye. His hair ain't black at all. I've seen the empty bottles."

"Oh," said Rose, deflated. "That's not an interesting secret at all." She thought it quite likely that half the performers who passed through Campion's were dyeing their hair, and the other half were probably using assumed names or had lost their original name. After all, Rose Campion wasn't even her real name, but the name Thomas had given her when he found her abandoned on Campion's doorstep.

Thinking about that conversation as she collected glasses, Rose began speculating in her head what her mother might have called her. She rather hoped it was a name from Shakespeare, like Viola or Portia. It would be a terrible disappointment to discover she was an Ethel or a Eunice. She chuckled to herself. Effie was certainly learning how to fool her and Rory. Thomas had been right – learning to be Gandini's assistant was good for Effie. In just a few days she had so much more confidence.

Rose glanced at the clock and hoped that Rory would come back soon. She missed her. Later, she and Rory would be performing their bicycle act. They did it much less often now that Rory and Edward spent more time at Silver Square.

After Edward and Rory had been reunited and Edward had taken charge of his inheritance, he and Aurora quickly decided that they didn't want to live at Easingford Hall in Yorkshire. Rose didn't blame them. She had visited Easingford, and as far as she could see there was nothing but sheep and moorland for miles around, which was fine for a holiday, but she wouldn't want to live there. After the constant clamour of London she had found the silence quite deafening.

Rose and Effie had been thrilled by Aurora and Edward's decision to make a permanent return to London. But even though he was appearing on the West End stage, which some considered a rackety profession, Edward was already moving in far grander circles, meeting daily with people who thought his acting was a charming pastime for a man with a considerable personal fortune, an extensive country estate, a London town house and one of the oldest titles in the land. Acting only added to Edward's glamour. Aurora was being swept into this orbit, and Rose saw less and less of her at Campion's.

An image crossed her mind of her and Aurora meeting accidentally one day many years hence, and of being like strangers with nothing to say to each other, even though for so many years their fates had been entwined, and for months they had squeezed top to tail in a bed at Campion's, laughing uproariously together.

She glanced back at the bar. Jem was standing by it, surrounded by a large group of men, including Gandini, and he appeared to be ordering them all drinks from Billy Proctor, who had just let another glass slip through his butterfingers. Billy Proctor had told Thomas he was an experienced barman, and had given Thomas references from The Anchor at Rotherhithe to prove it, but he barely seemed competent. Rose wondered if Thomas had actually taken up the references. Billy handed Jem four glasses of brandy and two tankards of ale. She frowned, wondering where Jem's new-found wealth had come from. It certainly wasn't from what he was being paid at Campion's, even though Thomas prided himself on paying all who worked for him rates above all but the biggest and most successful music halls. She wondered whether Thomas had noticed that Jem was flashing the cash around.

The door swung open and Aurora, Edward and Lydia walked in together, followed by Amy. Rose's mouth almost dropped open. Aurora was dressed like a smart young society lady in a sapphire silk tea gown edged with navy damask. Her outfit was completed by navy silk gloves and a chic matching little bonnet. She looked like a small replica of Lydia, who was also dressed in shades of blue, and she would not have been out of place on the streets of St James. Aurora hadn't spotted Rose, and Rose didn't call out a greeting, but she watched as the party progressed across the hall, attracting lots of interest. As they passed the bar, she thought she saw Gandini give an almost imperceptible nod towards Amy, who was lagging behind the main party looking glum in her dull mustard dress. Rose's eyes came back to rest on Aurora. She couldn't help thinking that Lydia's recent appearance in Edward's life was hastening the process of Aurora moving out of Campion's and settling permanently in Silver Square. She thought you'd have to have your eyes shut not to notice just how besotted Edward and Lydia were with each other.

She was in such turmoil that she barely registered the voice at her side.

"It's Rose Campion, isn't it," said a young man wearing a bowler hat and a creased tweed jacket. He had a trim little moustache and sharp terrier-like eyes. He nodded around the auditorium. "Another packed house, I see. Since the Doomstone was stolen, Campion's has been overflowing every night."

"Long may it continue," said Rose tersely.

"You were here, weren't you, on the night the Star of the Sea was stolen?"

"Yes," said Rose impatiently, piling glasses on to her tray. The man was obviously a reporter. "I was here, and like everyone else I didn't see anything. Not a thing, so I can't help you."

The man shook his head. "Strange that, ain't it? It's very convenient that everybody at Campion's was struck blind on the very night the Doomstone was stolen."

"If it has been stolen," said Rose darkly, her mind still on Rory in that silk dress. Rory was transforming into a lady more and more each day.

"What do you mean?" asked the man.

Rose shook her head impatiently, eager to get rid of the man. She felt his attention like a buzzing fly that she longed to bat away quickly. "Well, the Doomstone is definitely missing, but do we know that it's definitely been stolen?"

The man's eyes brightened. "You mean it could be an inside job?"

Rose laughed derisively as if she thought the man was being stupid, and shook her head as she expertly balanced the last few glasses on the tray. She was keen to go backstage and find Rory.

"I think," she said scornfully, "we can safely assume that whoever took the diamond was in the hall that night, don't you? After all, it's not as if the Doomstone could have been spirited away by magic, is it?" She stalked off, leaving the man, who immediately got out his notebook and began scribbling in it feverishly.

Thinking no more of the conversation, Rose took the glasses back to the bar and put them carefully on the polished mahogany surface.

"There you are, Billy, I've collected these for you," she said. He didn't offer a grunt of thanks. She turned to head off backstage when there was an almighty clatter and the sound of broken glass. Billy had knocked the entire tray off the bar.

"It's all your fault," he snarled. "You shouldn't have left them balanced so precariously. You better clear it up; you can see we're rushed off our feet here."

Rose sighed and picked up the broom. She was furious with Billy Proctor, but she didn't want to make a scene.

7

Aurora and Rose, the latter wheeling the daisy-sprigged green bicycle that they used in their act, ran off the stage together. The audience were still roaring their approval. The girls had been doing their bicycle act for almost six months now but the audience never seemed to tire of it, and Rose made sure that they kept on making little changes so it was never exactly the same and stayed fresh. Thomas had reminded her that if an audience liked an act enough, they didn't seem to mind even if they had seen it over and over.

As the Rubber Rubies, a pair of contortionists, ran past the girls and on to the stage to do their routine, Aurora swept the boy's cap from her head and her rusty brown hair tumbled down over her shoulders. She rubbed at her britches. The rough material was making her thighs itch in the heat from the gaslights.

"That's a terrific little act you've got there," said Inspector Cliff, stepping forward from the shadows and making Rory jump. Rose thought that the inspector was a bit like a cat, prowling around watchfully and suddenly appearing in places where you'd least expect him.

"We do our best," said Rose cheerfully, peering out into the auditorium. She could see Lydia and Edward at a centre table near the front. They were gazing at each other rather than at the stage. She glanced at Rory. Her friend had said nothing about her father and Lydia's blossoming relationship and Rose sensed that it was off-limits. She wondered if Rory realised quite how infatuated the pair were with each other even though they had only met just over a week ago.

"It's fascinating, isn't it," said the inspector turning to Aurora, "the way the people watching know that you are a girl and yet believe you are a boy when you're on stage."

Rory nodded. "That's the point. They enjoy the fact that they know. They don't feel that they're being deceived because they're already one step ahead. It's what makes it fun for them."

"Have you ever seen Vesta Tilley perform, Inspector?" asked Rose. The inspector nodded. Vesta Tilley was the toast of the music halls, and had been dressing up as a boy and singing since she was very small. "Well," said Rose, "when Vesta first began dressing up as boy, audiences thought that she really was a boy, and they didn't like her act at all. It was only when she changed her name to Vesta, which is clearly a girl's name, and began being introduced as Miss Vesta Tilley, so it was clear to audiences that she was a girl pretending to be a boy, that she found success."

"Interesting," said the inspector. "I suppose, in your world, people are always pretending to be somebody they're not."

Rory frowned. "Of course," she said. "We're all performing or acting when we're out there." She nodded towards the stage.

"Yes," said the inspector. "I realise that. I was thinking more about when people are off stage rather than on stage. That they may pretend to be something they are not."

Rory looked confused. "You mean you think I

might only be pretending to be me?" Then she added indignantly, "I'm Edward's daughter. It's been proven beyond doubt. I'm not an imposter. Although..." The others looked at her expectantly. Rory blushed quite crimson and said, "...although when I was out with Edward and Lydia in Hyde Park this afternoon wearing all that finery I did feel like a complete fraud. I look at Lydia, and whatever people say about her, and that she might not have born to it, you can see that being a lady comes naturally to her." Rory sighed heavily. "But me? I feel as if I'm just playing a part or conning people, and that they will see through my silk dress and bonnet and start pointing at me and saying, 'She's just a little guttersnipe who was dragged up by that blackmailing con-woman, Lizzie Gawkin, in the music halls.'"

Inspector Cliff bowed gallantly and took her hand. "Miss Aurora, if I may say so, I thought you were the one who looked every inch a lady when I saw you arrive at Campion's earlier."

"That's kind of you to say, Inspector," said Rory graciously. Then she grinned wickedly. "But those silk bonnets aren't half itchy on a hot day like today." All three of them laughed, and

Rose felt relieved. Maybe she wasn't losing Rory quite as quickly as she had thought.

"Inspector, Campion's has always been full of people pretending they are something or somebody they're not. After all, I'm not really Rose Campion. I'm just a baby who was abandoned here without even a name. But that's one of the reasons I love Campion's. It lets people be whoever they want to be. It can be a haven. And if they're not quite who they say they are – well, often they have a good reason for it. They're not trying to con anyone else out of anything – they're just looking for a place where they can be safe and be themselves."

"You love Campion's very much, don't you, Rose?" said the inspector quietly. Rose nodded vigorously. "You must have been very worried when Thomas's investments failed and it looked as though he would lose Campion's if he couldn't raise a great deal of money very quickly."

Rose was suddenly as alert as a rabbit sensing a fox. Maybe the inspector was less of the fool that the newspapers would have him be, and was actually being very clever hanging around Campion's, always watching, and engaging people in conversation when they weren't expecting it. She glared at him. "You don't think that Thomas…You couldn't possibly think…?!" She shook her head as if she had never heard such stupidity. "Thomas hasn't got a crooked bone in all his body." She drew herself up indignantly. "You'd do far better to look elsewhere, Inspector, and spend your time observing those who are quite obviously pretending to be something that they are not."

The inspector followed her gaze out through the auditorium to the heaving bar, where the customers were four deep waiting for their drinks and Billy Proctor was looking very flustered. He gave a wry little smile.

"I think that you are very observant, Rose," he said softly. But Rose had already turned on her heel and stalked away.

8

It was later the same evening. The final bows had been taken, the staff were clearing the bar area and the stage, and the sweltering day had turned into a balmy night. Any of Campion's staff or performers who weren't required were sitting out in the yard. A man had come by selling penny licks from a cart and everyone was enjoying the fast-melting ice crystals on their tongues. Effie was busy sketching their faces, quick drawings that somehow captured not just the features of the person but something of their spirit. Edward took a final lick of his ice and disappeared back inside, no doubt looking for Lydia, who had said that it was too hot outside and that she wanted to talk to Stratford-Mark to plan her debut. The portly Stratford-Mark kept appearing red-faced, perspiring heavily and unannounced at Campion's whenever Lydia was there with Edward. Rose wondered if he was jealous of the younger man, and that was the reason he was so watchful of this blossoming relationship. Perhaps he had romantic yearnings for Lydia himself? Or maybe he had other reasons for his watchfulness. In recent days it had felt increasingly as if everybody at Campion's was watching everyone else. It was just Edward and Lydia who had eyes only for each other. Rose had to admit that she had initially thought Lydia might only have eyes for Edward because of his wealth and title, but unless Lydia was a consummate actress she really did seem to be as smitten with Aurora's father as he was with her.

Gandini smacked his lips in satisfaction as his ice disappeared. "It's the taste of my boyhood. And the taste of the sea. When I was a child we went to Southend for our holidays. There was a little café run by a delightful family of Italians, the kindest people in the world, and they had a cart on the seafront selling penny licks, run by the oldest son, who was blind. They were the most delicious ices, and although the seller was blind nobody ever tried to cheat him. They trusted him to sell the best ices and he trusted them to pay him the fair price. That is how the world should be. For five happy summers he let me help him and his wife, before my mother said I was too old to play shopkeeper and I had to learn my trade." He sighed. "I would love to recover the innocence of that time, but life and love makes fools of us all." He looked sad. "I would so have treasured being an ice-cream maker, bringing nothing but pleasure and good to the world."

Rose was about to say that Gandini's magic tricks brought pleasure to people, when she saw Amy looking at Gandini with a frown, and then Effie spoke excitedly.

"That man's still there! Leastways he was a few years back. Me ma and me went for a day trip to Southend. Everyone round Shoreditch way used to call it Whitechapel on Sea. It was luverly. One of the nicest days of me whole life. It was before me ma's accident and we…" She trailed off sadly. Rose saw Amy shoot Effie a sympathetic look, and she warmed to the quiet, gawky girl in her ugly yellow dress.

"Lifts the spirits to be by the sea," said Lottie

quickly. "I should know, I was raised in Deal. I still sometimes fink I can 'ear the sea when I put me 'ead on the pillow and shut me eyes at night." And she broke into the chorus of a popular ditty about the delights of the seaside, and everyone sang along for a few bars.

"I've never seen the sea," said Rose wistfully.

"You're deprived. We should take a day trip on the train," said Aurora. "Where shall we go?"

"Brighton," said Jem. "That pier is one of the seven wonders of the world."

"Southend is better," piped up Amy, and everyone looked at her, because she so rarely spoke. "Gandini is right. Southend is the very taste of the sea. And you can get right away from the crowds if you walk a bit to the north where there are little brightly coloured fishermen's cottages, and oyster dredgers and the cockle sheds. One day I'm going to live there and be free, and feel the salt spray on my tongue every single day. And I'll eat a penny lick bought from the blind man every day too."

Everyone laughed, and the girl's eyes were shining as if she was lit from within and had suddenly come fully alive. Rose was about to ask her more, when Lydia's voice could be heard calling for Amy. The girl sighed, pushed back her red-gold hair, stood up and walked reluctantly inside, and the conversation broke up. There was something about her resigned demeanour that made Rose wonder whether Lydia was always kind to Amy.

Rose, Effie and Aurora moved away from the main group and perched themselves on two upturned buckets and a broken chair by the open gate. Ophelia, the cat, jumped on to Rose's knee. Aurora picked up some discarded balls and started to juggle, a skill that she had never grasped and showed absolutely no sign of mastering now. Effie diligently practised palming a coin as Rose indignantly told her what Inspector Cliff had said about Thomas and Campion's.

"It's outrageous," said Rose resentfully, "that he can even think that Thomas might be involved in any way with the theft of the Doomstone."

"He didn't actually say Thomas had stolen the diamond," said Aurora soothingly as she dropped all three balls, the noise making Ophelia dig her claws into Rose's lap.

"No," said Rose, "he didn't. But that's what he implied. Or that Thomas had allowed

Campion's to be used for some shady purpose and that's how he found the money to save the hall from those grasping bankers. But we know that's not how he found the money."

"How did he get it then?" asked Effie, looking interested. Aurora looked warningly at Rose. They both knew that as soon as Edward had come into his inheritance he had given Thomas the money; Thomas had immediately insisted that it must be a loan, not a gift, and was already paying it back. But neither man wanted the arrangement widely broadcast.

"He managed to borrow it," said Rose shortly. "I just hope that he's explained that to the inspector."

"We all know that Thomas isn't the guilty party," said Rory, "but we've never really had a chance to discuss who we think did steal the Doomstone."

"Well, it weren't me," said Effie quickly. Rose laughed.

"None of us think it was, Effie."

"Don't you believe it," said Effie darkly. "Mud sticks. Some people say once a prigger, always a prigger. That you can't change your ways."

"Do you really believe people think that about

you, Effie?" asked Rory.

"I dunno," said Effie sadly, "but Lottie said she heard one of them ballet girls tellin' that Billy Proctor 'bout my history, and how me mum is in Holloway. If she told 'im, she probably told the inspector and the whole of bloomin' Southwark." Rose saw Rory blush, and she guessed that Lydia probably also knew all about Effie's background.

"I wish I'd been there," said Rose furiously. "I'd have soon put them both right. But you shouldn't worry, Effie. Thomas will have told the inspector that he trusts you with his life."

"Yes," said Effie darkly, "but what if the inspector don't trust Thomas? If that's the case, what he says won't be worth sixpence." Rose and Rory looked at each other. Effie was right.

"It's all the more reason," said Rose, "why we need to think hard about who might really be responsible for the theft of the Doomstone." She stroked Ophelia under her chin. "Bet you know who did it, puss. You were there, under the table. I bet you saw everything." She looked at the others. "I reckon it could be Billy Proctor. We don't really know anything about him, and he was leaning over the table delivering some drinks just at the point that the Doomstone went missing."

"But if it was him, don't you think he'd have skipped Campion's immediately after? Why's he still here if he's the thief?" asked Aurora.

Effie nodded. "Anyways, Rosie. You've seen how clumsy he is. Reckon it'd be way beyond 'im to carry a tray and prig the diamond at the same time."

Rose smiled. It was hard to think of Billy Proctor with his butterfingers having the necessary sleight of hand to steal the Doomstone, but maybe his clumsiness was all an act. Maybe he wasn't all he seemed. Rose glanced over to the stage door, where Jem had started a card game with a couple of the stagehands. They were each betting against their hands and, judging by the big pile of coins by his side, Jem was winning. One of the stagehands threw down his cards in disgust and tossed Jem a coin.

"You've got the luck of the devil, Jem Dorries. I ain't playing no more." He walked away.

"You don't think...?" said Effie doubtfully as she followed Rose's gaze. She stopped as if she couldn't bear to say more.

"Surely not!" said Rory, shaking her head. "Jem is Campion's family."

Rose frowned. "He is. But he has been flush since the night the Doomstone went missing. Throwing it about too." She shook her head. "But I can't believe that Jem is responsible."

"Who else could it be?"

"Not Gandini, he was never close enough," said Rose.

Effie nodded. "Can't have been him what filched it. Not unless he had an invisibility cloak so he could get up close to Lydia."

"Amy?" asked Rose.

Effie shook her head and Rory looked shocked. "Not very likely, Rose. She's such a nervous little thing, hardly a criminal mastermind."

"I like her," said Effie. "When she gets the chance she watches me rehearse with Gandini."

"I thought he didn't like anybody watching?" asked Rose curiously.

"He don't," said Effie. "But he don't seem to mind Amy. Maybe it's because she's so quiet you don't know she's there. I've never heard them exchange a word, but he seems fine with her being there."

"What about Stratford-Mark? Everyone says

he has money troubles."

"Sitting too far away from Lydia," said Rose.

"If we can discount them all, it must be that man you saw, Rose, the one who told us about the Doomstone in the first place at the theatre," said Aurora.

Rose frowned. "But if he was planning to snaffle the Doomstone later in the evening, why draw attention to himself by telling us about it? But I suppose it does seem the most likely explanation," she said, as Ophelia jumped off her lap, wandered a little way off and began delicately cleaning her ears. "The only other person close enough to steal the Doomstone from Lydia's neck was Edward, and we all know it's as mad to think it was him as it would be to think it was Thomas."

"Unless of course," said Rory with a wicked smile, "Edward has been deceiving us all along, and all that time he was in America he was only pretending to be an actor and really he was a jewel thief."

"Likely story," laughed Effie.

Rose nodded. "It appears that the only one who really knows the truth of what happened to the Doomstone is Ophelia."

"Ophelia? Who is this Ophelia who knows the truth about the Doomstone?" asked a sharp voice with a distinct American twang behind them. They swung round. It was Lydia. She was right behind them, standing by Edward's side as pale as a pearl, her eyes alert and darting. The three girls burst out laughing.

"It's the cat," shrieked Rory. "Ophelia is the Campion's cat."

"Oh," said Lydia. She placed her hand against her chest as she said lightly, her accent all but gone and with a twinkle in her eye, "Maybe our good Inspector Cliff would like to interview this Ophelia. Maybe information supplied by the cat would advance his investigation, which to date doesn't appear to be making the slightest bit of progress."

Edward opened his mouth to say something, but at that moment there was a shout from the stage door and Thomas appeared, waving a newspaper.

"Rose! Rose!" he roared. "Have you seen this?" Rose stood up, shocked by Thomas's tone. He hardly ever shouted, and never at her. Out of the corner of her eye she saw Inspector Cliff, who she hadn't noticed was out in the yard, watching closely. She clocked Gandini and Amy, who suddenly appeared together at the stage door by the inspector's side. Some of the stagehands, who had heard Thomas's shout and were agog to know what was going on, pushed past them and out into the yard, followed by Billy Proctor, who sauntered over to the wall and leaned against it looking on in interest. Only Tobias Fraggles was looking in the other direction, his eyes fixed on Lydia. Aurora said that he reminded her of a faithful dog, the way he followed Lydia with his eyes. All this happened in a blink and then Thomas was upon her and waving the newspaper in her face. It was the first edition of a widely read paper that specialised in scandal and gossip. The headline read: "Missing Doomstone: Inside Job or Elaborate Hoax?"

Rose gasped. But it was as she started to read the story that her hands began to shake. "Earlier this evening Rose Campion, daughter of Thomas Campion of Campion's music hall, scene of the theft of one of the world's most valuable diamonds, the Doomstone, told our reporter that in her opinion it was an inside job. 'The Doomstone is missing, but do we know it's been stolen?' Miss Campion told our reporter coyly, and she made no denial when challenged as to whether she thought somebody from Campion's was responsible for the loss of the jewel, which has a curse attached to it. Instead Miss Campion declared that somebody from inside the building must have been responsible for its disappearance." The report then continued snidely: "It is well known that earlier this year Thomas Campion faced financial embarrassment and that creditors were poised to take control of Campion's music hall, when he miraculously found the money, believed to be a substantial sum, to pay off all his debts. Nobody knows where the money came from to save the ailing hall from falling into the hands of creditors and Mr Campion from falling into a debtors' prison. Since then Campion's appears to have gone from strength to strength, but industry insiders say that Campion's must still find it hard to compete with bigger and smarter music halls. A source, who did not want to be named, suggested that the disappearance of the Doomstone might simply be an elaborately stage-managed hoax designed to attract publicity for the music hall and boost audience numbers.

Rose Campion verified that the disappearance of the Doomstone had been excellent for business, confirming that the music hall has been packed every night since the Doomstone was stolen. 'Long may it continue,' said Miss Campion."
Rose lowered the paper feeling sick. Everyone's eyes were on her.

"I didn't... I wouldn't..." she whispered. But was that true? She had spoken to the reporter, even though he had twisted her words and misinterpreted what she had meant.

"Oh, Rosie, Rosie," said Thomas. "Are you trying to ruin me?"

"Oh, Thomas, of course not," cried Rose, tears falling down her cheeks.

"Come," said Edward, putting his hand on both Thomas's and Rose's shoulders and guiding them back towards the stage door. "Let's go inside and discuss this. Thomas, you know that Rose loves Campion's as much as you do, and would never do anything to threaten its future. This must all be a terrible mistake." He appeared to be looking straight at Inspector Cliff. "And, publicity stunt or no publicity stunt, we all know, Thomas, that you had nothing to do with the disappearance of the Doomstone.

It's ridiculous. As ridiculous as thinking that Lydia stole the diamond from around her own neck, or that I spirited it away."

9

Two days later, a subdued Rose and a nervous Effie stood holding hands and looking across the road at the forbidding entrance of Holloway Prison as they waited for several horse and carts and cabs to pass. Edward, Thomas and Mr Cherryble were standing just behind them. Thomas rested his hands lightly on both the girls' shoulders and pulled them back a little as a carriage lashed by, kicking up a spray of dirty water from the gutter. Thomas left his hand on Rose's shoulder and gave it a quick little squeeze. She was grateful. She knew it meant they were back to normal. She hated to think that she might have done anything to throw suspicion on Thomas, however unintentionally.

"He twisted my words to suit his own theory," Rose had explained tearfully in Thomas's study.

Thomas had shaken his head. "It's what these reporters do. It's why I told you not to talk to them." He sighed. "I don't know, Rosie. You're supposed to be the one with all the brains."

"I'm so sorry, Thomas, I wasn't thinking. I know it's no excuse but I was distracted."

"Listen," said Edward calmly, "there's probably no real harm done. Inspector Cliff isn't going to go round making any arrests on the basis of speculation in a downmarket rag."

Thomas had sighed. "I'm sure you're right, Edward. And it's not as if I have anything to hide. But the inspector makes me nervous the way he lurks here all the time watching, like a hunter just waiting for his prey to make a mistake." He looked at Rose and gave a glum smile. "Just don't go round talking to any more reporters."

Rose had nodded. "I won't. I promise."

Rose looked up at Holloway looming out of the yellowish afternoon haze. There was a strong smell of cabbages and drains. The prison resembled an unpleasant castle in a particularly nasty gothic novel. It looked as if it would be infested with bats and spiders and its walls would be damp with sadness.

Rose shivered and she felt Effie clutch her hand tighter. It was a horrible place. Rose had never known her birth parents, and she had sometimes envied Aurora for finding her father and Effie for the fact that she had a mother, albeit one incarcerated in Holloway Prison for stealing a watch, a crime that she hadn't actually committed. Effie's mum, Iris, had taken the blame for the theft to save Effie – who had been coerced into stealing by the malevolent Josiah Pinch – from going to prison. It had been an extraordinary act of motherly love but it had left Iris behind bars. Rose wondered if it was far worse to be living just a few miles apart like Effie and her mum, but quite unable to see each other, than having no mother at all.

For Rose, her lack of a mother felt like a dull pain that never went away, but which she had learned to live with, like an unpleasant headache. But she knew that Effie loved her mother fiercely and once, when Effie had been particularly down and was confiding in Rose, she had said that being constantly separated from her mother felt like having a small animal inside her gnawing at her heart with razor-sharp teeth.

"Yer know, Rosie, sometimes I think I might just drop down stone dead overcome by the pain an' longing to see her and have her arms round me again. A mother's hug is different from any other hug in the world." She had seen Rose's face. "Oh, Rosie, I'm sorry. I forgot. You don't know what it's like."

Rose had put her arm around Effie and said, "Oh, Effie, I'm the lucky one. Unlike you, I don't know what I'm missing." But she had still felt a pang at her own motherless state, and the fact that, unlike Effie, she had no idea who her mother had been and wouldn't have known her if she passed her in the street.

Rose knew that no one would be allowed to accompany Effie when she was taken to the sanatorium in the women's part of the gaol, where she would be briefly reunited with her sick mother, but she had wanted to come to support Effie as best she could and be there for her afterwards. Aurora would have come too but she had been carried off protesting by Lydia who wanted to take Rory to tea at Lady Fitzcillian's house in Mayfair, and then on to a rehearsal at the Pall Mall where Lydia was preparing to play Lady Macbeth, which Rose thought was the most improbable piece of casting she had ever heard. Lydia was always so sweet. Effie had challenged Aurora to bring back cakes for her and Rose.

"You can slide them into your knickerbockers. But be careful not to squash them. Me mum won't believe that I'm goin' to eat a pastry from Lady Fitzcillian's Mayfair residence. She'll be impressed I move in such lardy-dardy circles."

Rose didn't want to be cynical about Lydia's proposed trip with Aurora, but she was pretty sure that Lydia's interest in Aurora extended only as far as Edward. But maybe she was being too distrustful. Everyone appeared enchanted by Lydia. Even Thomas seemed quite charmed, and Rose couldn't help thinking back to that moment in Edward's dressing room, when Lydia looked as if she had been struck by a thunderbolt, to know that Lydia's feelings for Edward were genuine.

They walked through the gap in the iron railings that surrounded the prison to the main entrance, which with its two stone turrets resembled a threatening medieval stronghold.

They passed under the stone archway and through a smaller door made of thick black wood studded with iron. Just inside was a gatehouse, where Mr Cherryble gave his and everyone's name and said that they had an appointment to see the governor of the women's part of the prison, Julia Devonish. Julia Devonish had a reputation as a reforming governor, and had spoken loudly and publicly about the harshness of the courts, and how many of the women who ended up locked up in Holloway were there because of adverse circumstances rather than wickedness, and that their punishment fell as much on the families and the children of the mothers locked up as it did on the women who had been caught and convicted of a crime.

"You're expected," said the man in the gatehouse, and he nodded to a woman dressed in a uniform of a dark-blue dress and cap. The woman had a bunch of keys attached to her leather belt. "Mrs Hardy is the senior matron here. She will take you to Mrs Devonish's office."

Mrs Hardy smiled at them and beckoned them to follow her. She stopped to unlock and allow them to pass through a heavy metal barred gate, which she then relocked. They were in a drab yard surrounded by the prison buildings with tiny slit windows. Mrs Hardy hurried them across the yard, selected another key from her bunch and opened a small wooden door, waiting until they were all on the other side before relocking it. She then led them up a small staircase and through another door that had to be unlocked and shut behind them. They stepped through into a long narrow corridor painted grey. From somewhere far away they could hear voices and the clang of keys on metal.

"This way," said Mrs Hardy, leading them around a corner. She came to a halt in front of an imposing panelled oak door. She opened the door. A woman sat behind a desk in a room lined with leather-bound ledgers. She stood up and smiled at the visitors, and pointed to another smaller oak door.

"Mrs Devonish says you are to go through. I will provide some refreshments for you all."

Mrs Hardy rapped on the door, and a low voice called, "Come in."

"Your visitors, ma'am," said Mrs Hardy with a bob, and she ushered them through.

"Mr Cherryble, how lovely to see you. Charles

sends his best wishes and hopes you will visit him at his club soon," said the tall woman who stepped forward to greet them.

Mr Cherryble made the introductions, and as he did so, Rose examined Julia Devonish covertly. She wasn't a beautiful woman, but she had a frank, kind and animated face and her gaze was direct. Her hair was cropped to a glossy nape-length raven bob – a daring cut for any woman, particularly one of her position and class.

"And this," said Mr Cherryble, "is Effie, who has come to visit her mother. We are so grateful that you permitted her this visit."

Julia took Effie's hand. "I would have known you immediately. You look so much like your mother. You must be longing to see her, and you must wait no longer. But I must warn you, Effie, you will find your poor mother much changed. She is very sick indeed. The consumption is ravaging her."

Effie gazed up at Julia, her eyes trembling with tears. "Is my ma dying?"

Julia put her arm around the girl's thin shoulders. "I could lie to you, Effie, but I won't patronise you by doing so. Your mother is very ill. The doctor does not think that she can live. You will have to prepare yourself for the worst. But she is looking forward to seeing you very much." She smiled gently. "I will get Mrs Hardy to take you to see your mother now, so you do not waste a minute and have the longest possible time together. Would you like me to come with you?"

Effie sniffed. "Rosie. I want Rosie to come with me."

Julia looked pained. "I'm afraid that is against the rules…" The conflict was clear on her face. Then she said firmly, "But rules are there to be broken, and I will take responsibility if there are any consequences. Mr Cherryble has told me that you are like sisters." She walked to the door and opened it.

"Mrs Hardy. Please take these girls to see Iris Madley in the sanatorium. Sister Havering knows that Mrs Madley is expecting her daughter today, and tell her I am sanctioning two visitors. Oh, and remind Sister Havering that Ruth Bray has an authorised visitor this afternoon. He is expected shortly." She watched them leave, before turning back to the men.

"Tea, gentlemen? And then I can bore you

with my pet schemes for prison reform. It is a scandal that we keep these poor women locked up like this."

10

Rose leaned against the grey wall in the narrow corridor, her eyes damp with tears. She had gone with her friend into the room where Effie's mother lay on a narrow iron bedstead.

Rose had been shocked to see how awful Iris Madley looked, propped up against two thin pillows. Her eyes were sunken in a face that was flushed with fever, but also shrunken and skeletal. Rose had pushed Effie towards the bed and murmured a greeting to Mrs Madley, but as soon as Effie had seized her mother's thin, wasted hand and covered it with kisses, Rose had withdrawn to the corridor, close enough if Effie wanted her, but far enough away to allow mother and daughter some privacy. She could hear their smothered voices: Effie's urgent and full of love, and her mother's desperate gasping replies intercut with terrible wracking coughing fits.

Rose paced miserably up and down the corridor. The kindly but clearly overworked Sister Havering had been called away to another room at the far end of the narrow passage as soon as she had taken the girls into Iris's room. Rose continued pacing, finally coming to a stop outside the room next to the one where Iris was lying.

As if sensing her presence a feeble voice called, "Is somebody there? Anyone? Please help a poor old woman if you are there?"

Rose looked around, wondering if she should go and seek help from Sister Havering. But there was no sign of her. The voice called again. Rose poked her head shyly around the door. A pale woman, her sandy hair lying in wisps around her face, lay on the bed, her breathing cracked and laboured. She eyed Rose with sharp, beady surprised eyes and gestured her to come closer.

"Help an old dying woman," she rasped pitifully.

Rose moved closer to the bed and a hand like a claw with a surprisingly strong grip caught her by the wrist. Rose had to resist the urge to break away, but she felt sorry for anyone locked up in this dreadful place.

"What's your name, dearie?" asked the woman. "Are you with that girl come to see Iris Madley?"

"Do you know Iris?" asked Rose.

"We were in the same room until she took a turn for the worse. Iris won't see out the night. One of life's losers, is Iris Madley. Is that her daughter?" Rose nodded. The woman's feverish eyes narrowed. "She's the one that works in that music hall, Campion's, isn't she?"

"Yes," said Rose. "We both do."

"I heard that Campion's was closing down."

"Well, you heard wrong," said Rose indignantly, shaking the hand off and wondering how this woman got her information, locked away here behind thick walls in Holloway.

The woman appraised Rose. "I like a girl with a bit of spirit. You must be the daughter, the foundling discovered on the steps and adopted by that Thomas Campion, the one with the bad money troubles."

Rose tried to disguise her surprise. How did this woman know who she was and about

Thomas's financial difficulties? It made her shiver.

"Thomas hasn't got any money troubles. That's all behind him. Campion's is thriving again."

"I'm sure that's true," said the woman, her rasping made worse by her undisguised excitement, "now he's got his hands on the Doomstone. That pretty bauble will fetch a pretty price."

"Thomas had nothing to do with the disappearance of the Doomstone," said Rose and she was almost shouting. "Business is looking up and it will take a turn for the better still when Gandini starts his run at the top of the bill."

The woman looked interested, like a bird about to swoop on a delicious worm it had spotted.

"Gandini?" She said the name as if she was chewing on it and enjoying the taste. "What an unusual name." Her clawed hand shot out again and she clutched at Rose's sleeve before Rose had a chance to step away. "Listen, dearie, you can do a dying woman a favour. I'll make it worth your while. I need you to get a message out for me…"

The woman tensed. The click of Sister Havering's shoes could be heard in the corridor. Rose seized the opportunity to pull her arm away. She took a step backwards just as Sister Havering's name was called and the footsteps receded. The woman beckoned her closer but Rose wasn't going to be caught again.

"I'm sorry, I must go," she stuttered, and so eager was she to get away, she almost ran towards the doorway.

"A pity," hissed the woman after her, all sign of illness gone. "You could have been useful to me, and I might have been useful to you, Rose Campion. More useful than you could ever imagine. I know things: things you'd like to know..." She paused and hissed like a snake: "Little lost foundling. Little Miss Nobody."

Rose didn't wait to hear more; she stumbled into the corridor, just as Sister Havering appeared at the other end. She felt quite shaken up. How could this woman be so well informed?

"Are you all right, Rose?" Sister Havering asked kindly. "You look flustered. Why don't you sit down." She indicated one of two hard wooden chairs and took the other herself, sinking into it like a woman relieved to rest her aching feet.

"I'm fine," said Rose, not keen to admit to her encounter with the woman. Julia Devonish had permitted her to accompany Effie as a favour. Rose felt certain it was against the rules for her to be talking to prisoners other than Iris Madley. She didn't want the prison to have any reason to refuse Effie a future visit. She felt stupid and reckless for allowing her curiosity to overcome her, and she felt oddly stained by her encounter with the woman.

Sister Havering's kind face was careworn. "It's a bad business. Iris Madley has gone downhill so fast. Sometimes I think it's not just the consumption but despair that's killing her. Perhaps seeing her daughter will help her rally. She talks about her little Effie all the time when she's got enough breath." The Sister sighed. "It's always the good ones who go, the ones like Iris Madley with soft hearts and plenty of regrets. Not like that duchess in the next room. She'll pull through. She has the constitution of an ox and a heart hammered out of iron."

"Duchess? Is she royalty?" asked Rose, opening her eyes wide.

Sister Havering gave a short laugh. "She's

criminal royalty. That's why she's called the Duchess. Thieved and murdered and maimed all her life on her patch down Bethnal Green way. She ran gangs of pickpockets and is said to have been the brains behind some major thefts in the city and the West End. That one's so crooked she could hide behind a spiral staircase."

Rose tiptoed to the door of Iris's room and peeped through the crack. Effie had clambered on to the bed, and mother and daughter were lying side by side, gently stroking each other's faces as if they were beyond the need for words.

"They all right?" asked Sister Havering. Rose nodded. "You do realise that you and Effie will both have to leave soon? They've already had longer than is allowed in the rules."

"Yes," said Rose. She knew that when the moment came to go, it was going to be terrible to try and prise Effie away from her mother. It might be the last time she would ever see her. As if trying to distract Rose from thinking of that cruel moment when she would have to tell Effie that time had run out and they must go, Sister Havering continued telling Rose about the Duchess.

"The Duchess is a ruthless one, no mistake.

It's rumoured that she killed her own son, the Gentleman Dipper, the king of the priggers, who legend has it had such exquisite manners that he sometimes apologised to his victims before he fleeced them. But he tired of the criminal life and wanted to go straight. Well, the Duchess wasn't having that. So she killed him and his little daughter too. Cut both their throats, and apparently laughed when she did it. Said he was no son of hers. They say their bodies are weighed down with bricks at the bottom of the Regent's Canal. It may not be true. Others say it was him who betrayed her and that's why she's rotting here. Still others say the rumour was all a ruse and the Gentleman Dipper is out there somewhere lying low until he can pull off the crime of a lifetime, and that the Duchess was in on it all along, and it was just bad luck she got nabbed by the Blues eight months back. She's a sly one, that Duchess. They say she has friends in high places, or knows things about them that they wouldn't want anyone on earth to know."

Rose saw the Sister glance out the window at the clock on one of the prison towers. She felt a desperate need to try and prolong the conversation.

"What's the Duchess's real name?"

"Ruth Bray, but she goes under many aliases. Susan Perks. Ruby Bonnar. Beth Honer. Eliza Proc—"

There was a sudden broken cry from the room. It was unmistakeably Effie's voice. Rose and Sister Havering rushed to Iris's bedside. Effie was holding her mother upright as if her very life depended on it. Iris was coughing, her breath coming in great shuddering gasps. It was clearly far more serious than the previous coughing fits. Sister Havering ran out the room, calling for help. The spasm suddenly seemed to pass. Iris was staring straight ahead, a look of quiet intensity in her eyes. She reached blindly for her daughter's hand and clasped it to her heart.

"Effie," she said, her voice rusted with grief. "I love you."

"I know, Ma," whispered Effie. "I love you too."

"Never forget that you have been loved Effie. So loved," gasped Iris, and the light seemed to fade from her eyes as she closed them and sank backwards on to the bed as if she had simply fallen into a sudden deep sleep. Only a telltale trickle of blood at the corner of her mouth told another story. Iris Madley was dead. Effie gave a long wail, the grief rising in a voice that sounded as if it belonged to somebody else, someone immensely old and sad. Rose knelt by the bed and put her arms around Effie, who buried her face in Rose's shoulder and sobbed uncontrollably. Rose had always thought it was a terrible thing to have no mother, but she could see from Effie's pain that it was a terrible thing too to have to deal with the grief of losing one.

It was a sad and shocked party that clambered into a carriage outside Holloway Prison. Thomas had lifted Effie up into the carriage as if she was a floppy rag doll and she lolled against Rose. She stared straight ahead, saying nothing. As the carriage rumbled away, Rose glanced backwards. She hoped that she would never have to see Holloway Prison again as long as she lived. She craned her neck further. Unless she was much mistaken, she was sure that she had just seen Billy Proctor walking into the prison. She frowned. What on earth could have brought him there? Julia Devonish had mentioned that Ruth Bray, or the Duchess as she was known, was expecting a visitor. Could Billy be that visitor? If he was, did it mean he was involved in the criminal underworld? Maybe the Duchess had orchestrated the theft of the Doomstone from Campion's from her prison cell. She certainly seemed to know a great deal about the place. Rose's heart gave a skip of excitement, but Effie's sobs made her banish the thought from her mind, and she directed all her attention towards her poor, broken friend.

11

Rose walked down the back corridor at Campion's towards the male dressing rooms, whistling to herself. She had some costumes to deliver, fresh from the laundry. This evening Effie would be appearing for the first time on the Campion's stage assisting the Illustrious Gandini, a debut that had been delayed because of her mother's death. Thomas had repeatedly asked Effie if she was sure that she still wanted to perform with Gandini, particularly as her mother's body had only been laid to rest in St Olave's burial ground two days ago. But Effie had been quite determined to go ahead.

"Me ma would have wanted me to," she told Rose and Thomas. "I told her I was goin' to be a magician's assistant an' she couldn't have bin prouder than if I told her I was going to be crowned the queen of England. She always loved the magic acts when we went to the Fortune in Hoxton. And I couldn't let Mr Gandini down."

"Well, just as long as Gandini is understanding of everything you've been through, and doesn't get upset if you get something wrong," said Rose.

"I don't reckon anything will go wrong," said Effie confidently. "Mr Gandini makes me plan and check everything over and over. He's a real stickler for that. He says that failing to prepare properly is exactly the same as preparing to fail, an' it's not worth the risk."

Hearing the word "risk", Thomas looked anxious. "You're not going to do the bullet trick tonight?" he asked with a frown.

"Nah," said Effie. "We're still working on that one. No room for any error there. We've got to be quite certain we've got it right. People have died tryin' it."

"I'm not sure it should ever be performed," said Thomas. "It's far too dangerous."

"Don't worry, Thomas," said Effie. "I'd trust Gandini with me life. He's a perfect gentleman and I ain't had nothing but kindness and patience from 'im. He won't do no trick that he ain't certain will work."

Rose shifted the costumes she had hanging over her shoulder and knocked on the dressing-room door. There was no answer. She pushed the door open and started to hang up the clean costumes on a rail. She could hear a low murmur of voices from the props room next door.

"You're being blind. You just won't see what's going on right under your nose," said an impatient voice that Rose didn't recognise. She couldn't even be sure if the speaker was male or female. She wondered who it was. The wall muffled and distorted the sound. Was it a woman or a man? She thought it could be Jem but she really wasn't certain. Maybe it was Lydia, who she thought she had spotted earlier in the bar.

"Things are not always what they seem. You should know that better than anyone," replied another voice. She was pretty sure this voice was male, but again, the wall made it hard to be sure. Maybe it was Billy, or Thomas. "Besides, we're in too deep now to get out. I've come up with a plan if things get hot that will get us all out of this nightmare. It involves you." Rose frowned.

She wished she could identify the voice.

"You're being a fool!"

"Keep your voice down; walls have ears," hissed the other person, and the voices dropped. Rose couldn't hear any more of the exchange. She walked out of the room and stopped by the storeroom. She was very curious to know who was talking inside but she didn't want to be caught eavesdropping. She was just about to turn the handle and fling open the door when Thomas appeared at the end of corridor and called out to her.

"Ah, Rosie! Be a dear and go and help wash the glasses at the bar ready for the rush this evening. Billy Proctor seems to have disappeared off the face of the earth for the last half an hour. I know you've been hard at it all afternoon and I would ask Lottie or Jem to lend a hand, but I can't find them anywhere either." Rose hesitated. She would love to know who was in the storeroom but Thomas was shooing her towards the bar. When she got a chance to double-back a few minutes later the storeroom door was ajar and the corridor outside was full of people, including Jem and Lottie. Lydia was talking in a low voice to Amy, and Gandini and Billy Proctor were in deep conversation.

"Hey, Billy," said Rose. "Thomas is looking for you. You're supposed to be on bar duty." Billy coloured, and pushed his way past her towards the bar. Rose followed him, and said quietly, "By the way, I spotted you going into Holloway Prison last Wednesday afternoon."

Billy's voice was terse. "You are quite mistaken, Rose. I've never been anywhere near Holloway. It must have been someone else."

"Oh," said Rose sweetly. "And I thought you were visiting the Duchess."

"Never heard of her," said Billy. But Rose could see that he was clenching his knuckles so tightly they had turned quite white.

* ✳ *

It was later that evening. Campion's was brimming over with crowds eager to see Gandini's return to the stage for the first time since the disappearance of the Doomstone. Rose and Rory peeped out from backstage into the Campion's auditorium. Edward had just arrived, hotfoot from performing Hamlet at the Pall Mall. Lydia came up behind him and murmured something in his ear that made him smile. Amy, who seemed to follow Lydia around like a faithful but discontented lamb glued to the side of a negligent shepherdess, was looking on stonily. With every day that went by she looked more ill at ease and grumpy. Stratford-Mark was bringing up the rear and he seemed more mournful than ever. Rumours were swirling around town that he was facing ruin within weeks, and that the Pall Mall would have to be sold unless he could come up with money to pay his debts almost immediately. Rose had overheard Edward and Lydia talking about it only the previous day.

"He may be a bad businessman but he genuinely loves that theatre; it's an obsession with him," said Edward.

"Just as you are for me," replied Lydia, looking deeply into Edward's eyes. "Don't worry about Stratford-Mark, Edward. I have every confidence he'll find a way to save the Pall Mall. That kind of passion always finds a way. It can't be thwarted."

Now Edward was looking anxiously around in search of Effie. "Am I too late to see Effie before she goes on? I wanted to give her a little present to mark her debut," said Edward, and he drew a small box out of his pocket and opened it. Inside nestled a small, perfect pearl, tied on a piece of black silk ribbon.

"She's upstairs in Thomas's office," said Rose. "Apparently Gandini likes to be on his own just before a performance, so Thomas said that if Effie wanted to be somewhere quiet, she could sit in his office. Rory and I were just going up to check that she's all right. We'll go up together. The pearl's beautiful, Edward."

As they entered the study, Effie turned to face them. She was ash-pale and her eyes were panicked.

"I can't do it, I can't go on," she said desperately. "I've forgotten everything Mr Gandini taught me. I'll ruin everything. An' everyone will laugh and say I'm just a little prigger who's got above meself and thinks she can be somebody by becoming a magician's assistant."

Edward stepped forward and took her hand. "Effie," he said gently. "It'll be all right. I know it will. Every single night just before I go on stage I think I've forgotten every word that Hamlet says. Some nights my mind's so blank that I can't even remember what my first line is, and I get into a terrible funk. But once I get out on stage, everything I'm supposed to say and do comes back miraculously. It will for you too. I promise. You're just suffering from stage fright. Everybody gets it. It's just that some people – and that's you and me – get it worse. But you will be fine."

"No I won't," said Effie despairing. "I can't even palm a coin. I've forgotten how. Look!" She took a coin in her hand, and as she tried to make it disappear her hands shook and she fumbled it, and the coin dropped to the ground. She picked it up, muttering to herself, and the same thing happened again. "See," she cried. "I've forgotten everything. I'm stupid and useless. Just like everyone said I was at school."

Amy bent and picked up the coin. "No, you're not stupid, Effie, and you haven't forgotten. I've heard you are very clever, a natural magician's assistant. You can do it, I know you can. Look, I'll show you," she said, and she rotated the coin and put it in her left palm with her right hand and quickly curled her fingers. When she opened her palm the coin had gone. "Now you try," she said kindly. "It's easy. Don't even try to think about it. Your fingers will just know what to do. They remember. Once they learn, the fingers never forget. I promise."

Effie took the coin and did exactly as Amy had demonstrated.

"Oh, Amy," she cried tearfully, "I can't thank you enough. You should be Mr Gandini's assistant, not me." She looked to the door. "Hello, Inspector, have you come to see me be a magician's assistant?"

Rose glanced over her shoulder. She hadn't noticed the arrival of Inspector Cliff, who was leaning against the doorframe watching them all. She wondered how long he had been standing there and whether he had witnessed Amy's expert magic demonstration. She also wondered where Amy had learned to do magic. It was almost as if they had just seen an entirely different Amy, confident and in control, from the one who crept after Lydia like a little ghost. She wondered which was the real Amy, and which the imposter.

The inspector smiled at Effie. "Effie, I've come to wish you—"

"No!" shouted Rose, Rory and Edward simultaneously.

"Don't say it, Inspector," screeched Rose. "Don't you know it's bad luck to wish anyone good luck just before they go on stage in a theatre or music hall?"

The inspector shook his head. "I had no idea." He turned to Effie. "But I'm very much looking forward to seeing you and Gandini working together." Then he turned to Amy. "You could be in a magic show yourself, Miss Hodgson. I had no idea you were so skilled."

"I'm not really. I just picked a bit up when I was in—"

But Lydia spoke over her loudly and cut her off. "Look, Effie, Edward has a present for you."

Edward gave Effie the box and when she opened it and saw the pearl, her eyes brimmed with tears.

"Oh, Eddie. It's so lovely. I'll be jest like a real lady. It's much more beautiful than that stupid Doomstone."

"It is," said Rose. "And it doesn't come with a curse attached either."

"No," said Edward. "It certainly doesn't. In fact, I hope that it will bring you all the good fortune in the world, Effie. You deserve it."

Thomas appeared at the door. "Effie, Gandini is asking for you. You must come downstairs. It's almost time."

The party started to walk downstairs, Edward

stopping to talk to Jem, who was waiting for him at the bottom, looking anxious. The two men walked to a spot where they would have a little privacy.

Rose glanced back as they walked towards stage right and the two men were in deep conversation, worry etched on both their faces as Jem waved his hands around as if denying something.

"I feel as if I'm going to me execution," whispered Effie, and Rose wasn't at all sure that she was joking. They met Gandini by the side of the stage. The magician had the demeanour of a recently deceased corpse that had been terrified to death. He was horribly pale, his forehead was slicked with sweat and his hands were visibly shaking. Rose and Thomas glanced at each other: Gandini was clearly suffering from something far worse than a bad oyster.

"Are you ready, little Effie?" he asked kindly, a tremble in his voice. "You are the best magician's assistant that Gandini has ever had. We will go out there together and make your mother proud," he said. A rivulet of sweat ran down the side of his face into his black beard.

"We will," said Effie firmly and she smiled

gently at the magician and took Gandini's shaking hand, all her nerves apparently evaporated, and squeezed it.

"I can't do it, I can't go on," said Gandini despairingly.

"Yes, you can," said Effie very calmly, her own nerves vanished as if she had been performing every single day of her life. "We can do this together, Mr Gandini. We'll lean on each other." There was a roll of cymbals and a puff of smoke on the stage. "Come," said Effie, like a parent leading a frightened child, and she stepped out on to the stage pulling the reluctant Gandini behind her. Rose's and Thomas's eyes briefly met. The Great Wizard of the North suffered from the worst stage fright that they had ever seen. The start of every performance must be pure hell for him. Rose wondered how he could possibly go on performing when stepping on to a stage was clearly such agony.

The audience yelled with delight. Gandini had taken the red silk handkerchief handed to him by Effie and stuffed it into his curled fist. Then, when he opened his fist, the silk handkerchief had disappeared and instead there was an egg in his palm. Effie had immediately produced a second red silk handkerchief and placed it over Gandini's hand containing the egg. Gandini passed his other hand over the handkerchief and Effie pulled away the red silk material to reveal a small fluffy chick. The audience gasped and burst into applause, drumming their feet so hard that Rose felt the gallery vibrate.

Within a few minutes of stepping on stage, all Gandini's stage fright seemed to evaporate and he was in total control. Thomas relaxed. Rose and the others moved into the auditorium for a better view. Lydia and Edward were sitting at a table near the stage with Stratford-Mark, but Rose, Aurora, Thomas and Amy had gone upstairs to the gallery, where they had a good view of the stage and the front of the auditorium. Rose winked at Aurora. They were thrilled that Effie was doing brilliantly. She seemed remarkably assured. Anyone would have thought that she had been a magician's assistant all her life.

Gandini and Effie were now doing a trick involving eggs and a bucket. They were going around the auditorium, and Gandini was plucking eggs from behind the ears of audience members. Gandini and Effie stopped in front of Inspector Cliff. Gandini reached behind the policeman's neck and produced a fluffy yellow chick, and then another and another. The audience guffawed with pleasure. They all knew he was the policeman who so far had failed to solve the crime of the missing Doomstone.

"Look a bit 'arder, Gandini, an' yer might find the Doomstone be'ind the peeler's neck," yelled one wag in the audience, and there were chortles of delighted laughter. Inspector Cliff was smiling too, but the smile was fixed, as if he knew that he was being made a fool of by being the focus of Gandini's attention.

Effie and Gandini moved back to the centre of the stage for a coin trick. Knowing that everything was going so well for Effie, Rose allowed her gaze to wander. She had half an eye on what was happening on stage, and half an eye on the audience. Billy Proctor was delivering some drinks to Edward and Lydia. Edward's hand was resting gently over Lydia's. Rose gave a quick sidelong glance at Aurora. She wondered if her friend had noticed. She could see that Stratford-Mark had seen the gesture – his eyes were fixed upon that hand. Rose frowned. Was Stratford-Mark jealous? Did he too harbour feelings for the beautiful Lydia? But she wasn't sure. The way he was looking sideways at his two stars, Edward and Lydia, suggested less unrequited love, more undisguised greed. Maybe, Rose wondered, he didn't see them as people – just tickets sold at the box office.

Distracted by that little drama being played out on the table below, Rose looked quickly back at the stage, and as she did so she saw Gandini reach up his sleeve and remove a coin. She was surprised to see him being so sloppy. But she was astonished when the crowd burst into applause. Even Thomas and Aurora were applauding loudly. But surely everyone must have seen what she had seen? Gandini had flunked the trick. But clearly they hadn't: they were all cheering wildly. She frowned. She suddenly thought back to what Effie had said about how closely related magic and prigging were, and how a pickpocket used misdirection so he or she could carry out their crime without anyone noticing what they were doing, including the person who was the mark. Could it be that everyone was looking so hard at what Gandini and Effie were doing, and trying to work out exactly how they were doing it, that they completely failed to notice what was going on under their noses? That perhaps you needed to look less hard to see the truth?

Her eyes flicked around the auditorium. She started. The man with the handlebar moustache who had spoken to her and Rory and Effie was in the audience again. He was much more soberly dressed – no sign of the peacock-blue waistcoat – but it was unmistakeably him. His tie offered a vivid flash of blue, and he was wearing a diamond tiepin that caught the light. Rose reckoned the Tanner Street boys would be eyeing up that tiepin. The man was next to Billy at the side of the auditorium, and there was something about the way they were standing side by side, and the way Billy whispered something in his ear, that made her think that they had a long-standing familiarity. She frowned. Campion's brought people of all backgrounds and classes together, but even so, you wouldn't expect a barman and a gentleman to be on such easy terms with each other. She decided she would race down the stairs at the end of the act and try to alert the inspector to the man's presence, and while she was about it, maybe she would have a word with him about Billy.

She was about to turn her eyes back to the stage when she saw Edward look towards the place where Billy and the man from the Pall Mall were standing together. The man gave Edward an understated thumbs-up, and Edward gave an almost imperceptible nod. Rose was disconcerted. It was almost as if some kind of signal was passing between the two men.

Her mind racing, she glanced back at the stage where the dove trick, now famed because of its association with the theft of the Doomstone, was once again being performed to the delight of the audience. Gandini had shown the audience the table before placing his fez upon it, and once again he was telling the audience to count the doves as they flew out of the upturned fez. Everyone's attention was focused firmly on the fez and the doves, which this time, to the evident pleasure of the audience, were not just white but all the colours of the rainbow. Although Rose was captivated by the doves she was also looking around the audience. She was not the only one. Her gaze met that of Inspector Cliff, and his eyes lingered on her for a second. She wondered whether Inspector Cliff was quite the fool that everyone took him for. Maybe in his own way he was as much of a magician as Gandini, skilled at seeming to be a little bit incompetent and unthreatening, when all the time he was building up a bigger picture, and a case against whoever had stolen the Doomstone. But that meant he must think that somebody connected with Campion's was responsible for its theft.

She glanced back at the fez and the table and, once again, perhaps because she was thinking about the inspector, she thought she saw something she shouldn't have seen: a tiny flicker of movement in the cloth covering the table. Gandini and Effie must have found a way of secreting the box of doves under the table after Gandini had shown it to the audience to demonstrate that there was no trickery involved. It was the only explanation. The final dove flew out of the fez to tumultuous applause and the birds flew in a circle around Gandini's head. It was the end of the act. Gandini and Effie took a bow before running off stage together. The audience continued to cheer loudly, drumming their feet on the wooden boards, making a sound like rolling thunder. But Gandini and Effie did not return. Rose frowned. Her heart began to beat faster. Why hadn't they come back? Was something wrong? She saw an anxious furrow in Thomas's brow.

But then, suddenly, there was a tiny puff of smoke from the fez and then another and another. The crowd fell silent again. Then a lop-eared rabbit suddenly poked its nose out of the hat and looked around, as if astonished to find itself on stage. The rabbit struggled out of the hat and on to the table. It sat for a second blinking as if with surprise, before jumping down off the table and hopping off stage. Only then did Gandini return to the most astonishing laughter and applause. He beckoned off stage and Effie joined him, holding the rabbit in her arms. Gandini put an arm around her shoulder and smiled broadly. Rose looked down into the auditorium: the man from the Pall Mall had disappeared as if he had been magicked away. Rose rushed down the stairs and pushed her way through the crowds to the door. She could see the man at the far end of the alley just getting into a hansom, and called out, but it had already pulled away. She turned, defeated, and as she went to go back towards Campion's she was surprised to see Lydia standing by the entrance, all alone, fanning herself. There were tears in her beautiful eyes. She rubbed them away in a manner that reminded Rose of a small angry child and tried to smile brightly at Rose.

"Lydia! Is everything all right? Can I get Edward for you?" asked Rose.

Lydia gave her a watery smile and shook her head. "No. I'm just being silly. I was overcome with emotion watching little Effie and Gandini doing their act together. They work in such harmony together."

Rose suddenly warmed to Lydia, seeing

how touched she had been by the triumph of the magician and Effie. "It's lovely to see Effie looking so happy after all that's happened to her."

"Perhaps her luck has changed. She is a most delightful magician's assistant," said Lydia. "Much better than…" She stopped as if censoring herself. She suddenly looked sad and wistful. "Sometimes I wish I could turn back the clock."

Rose hesitated and then she said boldly, "If you turned it back too far, it would mean that you would never have met Edward."

"Edward is the best thing that's ever happened me," said Lydia, and suddenly she looked very young and utterly defenceless. "He's my second chance. I love him with all my heart, and I know I don't deserve him." She bit her lip and her eyes filled with tears again. "I'm mad with love for him. He's a good man – I would do anything for him. Even give up my own life." She said it so fiercely that Rose felt both touched by her passion and disconcerted by the strength of it. She felt embarrassed that Lydia, who she hardly knew, was confiding in her.

Rose squeezed Lydia's hand. "I must go," she

said, and slipped back inside.

When she got back to the gallery, the applause was still rumbling like thunder. It was the longest standing ovation that Campion's had ever witnessed. Rose and Thomas grinned at each other. Together, Gandini and Effie could turn out to be Campion's most successful act ever. But Rose knew it would only happen if Gandini could overcome his stage fright sufficiently to perform regularly, and having glimpsed the crippling fear in his eyes, that was by no means certain. Rose had known plenty of performers who had become so paralysed by stage fright that they had to abandon their stage careers entirely. From what she had seen tonight, she thought that Gandini might be one of them.

It was late, very late, but nobody wanted to go home. Everyone knew that it had been a landmark evening for Campion's and they didn't want it to end. Only Jem was absent, slinking off as soon as his work had finished. Everyone else wanted to keep toasting the evening's success, and in particular Gandini's prowess and Effie's debut. It was another hot London evening, and people were sitting outside in the yard. Gandini looked relaxed and happy. There was no sign of

145

the terrible nerves that had afflicted him earlier.

"You were magnificent, Effie. I couldn't have done it without you. You are the best magician's assistant I've ever had."

"Have you had lots of magician's assistants, Mr Gandini?" asked the inspector, who once again had appeared stealthily. "Perhaps when you were in America you had others?"

Gandini gave the inspector an amused smile. "It is no secret that I have spent time in the New World, Inspector, and yes of course I have had other assistants. But none who can calm me quite like Effie. She is my saving grace."

"Oh, Mr Gandini, America! How exciting. You might have met both Edward and Lydia while you were there. They were both in America," said Effie eagerly.

"America is a very big place, Effie," said Gandini with a smile, "but if I had met either Edward or Lydia I know I would remember them." Lydia flung Gandini a cryptic look. Amy gave an odd little smile.

"I have an announcement to make," said Inspector Cliff. The entire yard fell silent. "Our investigation into the disappearance of the Doomstone and the attempted murder of Miss

Duchamps has made considerable progress. An arrest is imminent. I will provide you all with more information by tomorrow afternoon at the latest. In the meantime, if anyone has anything that they wish to tell me, or information they wish to share, I would advise them to do so now in their own interests. Or it may reflect very badly upon them." The inspector looked serious, and his eyes flicked around everyone present. Rose watched. Some, like Gandini, met his eye. Others, like Effie and Amy, looked uncomfortable. Lydia seemed as serene as a calm sea, and gave the inspector a beatific smile, and then winked at Tobias Fraggles – an oddly flirtatious response in the circumstances, thought Rose. Billy Proctor looked as if he was feigning boredom. Lottie, Tessa and some of the other ballet girls giggled nervously. Edward and Thomas were both frowning and exchanged a quizzical glance, and lots of people simply looked as if they were trying to disguise their excitement because it would be deemed inappropriate.

Rose still found it hard to believe that somebody present could have been responsible for the theft of the Doomstone – except perhaps

Billy Proctor. She wondered if Inspector Cliff really was as close to making an arrest as he implied – or was he just getting desperate at his lack of progress and trying to smoke the culprit out?

The announcement put a damper on the evening. Everyone began to gather their things and make their good nights.

"Edward," said Rose, suddenly remembering the mysterious man from the Pall Mall who had been at Campion's earlier, just as he had on the night of the disappearance of the Doomstone. "Who was that man with the bright-blue tie and diamond tiepin that you nodded at during the performance? He was standing by Billy Proctor."

Aurora, who was standing by Rose, looked at her father expectantly. He glanced at her, a trace of anxiety in his gaze.

Edward shrugged and his voice was quite tight. "I didn't nod at any man, Rose. You must be mistaken."

"I must have been," said Rose, but she was sure that she wasn't and she was puzzled by Edward's response. He was normally so open about everything.

Edward strode over to where Gandini was

standing, just as a boy turned up in the yard asking for Gandini, who took a note from him, read it and frowned, and then murmured something to Edward.

Edward bit his lip, and then called, "I'll get you a cab, Lydia. I have business with Thomas."

"I'll get my wrap," said Lydia, and she disappeared through the stage door with Amy in tow. Gandini followed them.

13

The next afternoon, everyone gathered in the auditorium at the request of Inspector Cliff. There was a low-level hum of excitement. Rose, Aurora and Effie had discussed the inspector's message and decided that it sounded much more like an order than a request.

"Maybe if you don't turn up the inspector will know you're the person he needs to arrest. But what if we all fail to turn up, what will he do then? Arrest all of us?" grinned Aurora.

"Well, I'm definitely going," said Effie, looking scared. "I don't want to be arrested and sent to prison."

"Nobody's going to arrest you, Effie," said Rose soothingly. "You haven't done anything wrong."

"I know I ain't," said Effie, nervously fingering the pearl around her neck, "but it don't stop me feeling guilty, as if I have done something I shouldn't and the inspector knows 'bout it."

Rose and Rory glanced at each other. They both knew that Effie was consumed with regret and guilt about her mother having saved her from prison. But Effie couldn't possibly have stolen the Doomstone.

"Listen, if the inspector is stupid enough to try and arrest you, Thomas and Rory and I will stop him. We promise. Even if we have to wrestle him to the ground and fling him in the trap under the stage," said Rose.

"Well, I think the whole thing is ridiculous," said Aurora. "If the inspector is confident he knows who stole the Doomstone, why doesn't he just arrest them and have done with it? Why make such a performance out of it, unless all this hanging around Campion's has given him a taste for the stage?"

"That's what Thomas said," said Rose. "I can never work out whether the inspector is stupider or cleverer than he's letting on."

They were sitting in the auditorium together, close to Gandini, who was looking gloomy, near to Lottie, Tessa, Belle Canterbury and some of the other ballet girls. He seemed as nervous as he did when he was about to go on stage. Rose looked around.

"Is anyone missing?" she asked.

"Edward's not here," said Aurora, "and there's no sign of Lydia or Amy either."

"Some of the mudlark children were at the stage door, and they said a flock of sheep had escaped on the bridge and caused chaos. Maybe they're held up because of it."

"They're not together," said Aurora shortly. "Edward had business in the city; Lydia is at the theatre with Stratford-Mark. She's supposed to be rehearsing the Scottish play." Theatrical superstition meant that nobody ever said the title of *Macbeth* in a theatre.

"Is she any good?" asked Rose. She was curious to see Lydia act.

Rory wrinkled her nose. "She looks lovely, but I'm not sure looking lovely is the point of Lady Macbeth. But then Stratford-Mark is hardly typical casting for a brave warrior."

Effie had been looking around. "There's no sign of Jem either."

"Or Billy Proctor," said Rose thoughtfully.

"Wonder whether he's done a runner. I've always had my suspicions about him. Maybe the inspector has arrested him and he's going to announce it."

Inspector Cliff had arrived and was talking to Thomas in a lowered voice. A look of consternation crossed Thomas's features. Then the inspector stepped on to the stage and held up a hand.

"Ladies and gentlemen, thank you for coming." He paused as Edward arrived, looking pale, flustered, and muttering apologies.

"I'm afraid that I have some bad news, which I know you will all find distressing. An accident has befallen Jem Dorries. He was found early this morning in an alleyway down Lant Street. He has been badly beaten up and is now in hospital, where his condition is a cause for concern." A buzz went round the room. Everyone liked Jem, who was easygoing and kind, and, when he had money in his pocket, always generous. Who could want to harm him?

"Jem's not going to die, is he?" asked Lottie, who, like several of the ballet girls, had tears in her eyes.

"He has been very badly assaulted," said the

inspector. "His condition is grave. But he may yet recover."

Rose looked around. Everyone was talking and the ballet girls were comforting each other. Edward had his head in his hands, Thomas looked pensive and Rose saw Gandini wipe away a tear. Who would ever have thought that the magician was so soft-hearted? Although, now she thought about it, Rose realised that she had seen the magician with Jem on several occasions, often playing cards together. She saw Edward and Gandini exchange an anxious glance.

Lottie called out, "Inspector, do you think the attack on Jem could be connected with the theft of the Doomstone and the attack on Miss Duchamps?"

The inspector opened his mouth to answer, but at that moment Lydia appeared, looking distraught, her hands fluttering as she pushed back locks of hair that had escaped from her elaborately arranged coiffure.

"Amy?" she cried, peering around the room. "Amy, are you here?"

"She's not here, Miss Duchamps," said the inspector calmly.

"Oh," whispered Lydia, and she suddenly looked deflated. "I hoped I would find her here safe and sound."

"Miss Duchamps, do you have any reason to fear for Amy's well-being?"

"She has disappeared. Little Amy is gone. She wasn't at the theatre this morning, and that's so unlike her that I knew at once that something was wrong. I thought maybe she was ill. So I sent a message to the address of her lodgings that she gave me. But it was most confusing because by return I had a note saying that she didn't lodge there and they had never heard of her. I know that the address is correct. She wrote it down for me in her own hand in case I ever needed to send her a message." She gazed into the inspector's face, her eyes huge and troubled. "It's so very odd. But I can't help feeling that something terrible must have happened to her. We are so fond of each other. I know she would never leave me without good reason."

Lydia burst into tears and rushed into Edward's arms. Tobias frowned. Edward's face looked shrunken, as if he had suddenly aged a decade.

"I feel so responsible for her," Lydia cried, and

she tilted her face towards Edward. Rose saw a flicker of emotion that looked like irritation, or maybe jealousy, cross Gandini's face. Rory looked away and Edward looked preoccupied, barely seeming to notice Lydia, which was unusual, thought Rose, because he was normally so attentive to her.

"When did you last see Amy?" asked the inspector.

"Me...?" stuttered Edward, and stopped as Lydia put a finger against his lips.

"I think the inspector is asking me," she said, a little too archly for the circumstances. "Last night. Here. Edward sent a boy to get a hansom for me soon after your announcement. He offered to get one for Amy to take her to Rotherhithe too, but she had already gone as she prefers to walk. I should never have let her go."

"Ladies and gentlemen, in the light of these developments, I'm going to call a halt to this meeting," said the inspector. "I am concerned about Miss Hodgson's well-being, particularly in light of what has happened to Jem. I'd like to talk to any of you who might have any further information about either Jem Dorries or Miss Hodgson, particularly as to exactly where Miss

Hodgson was lodging."

Rose raised her hand. "Effie and Rory and I might be able to help you. We took Amy back to her lodgings on the night the Doomstone was stolen."

"Then I'd like to talk to the three of you as a matter of urgency," said the inspector, "and anyone else who might have any information." He gazed around the room, as if examining the faces of everyone present. His eyes were as watchful as a cat's.

14

Rose, Effie and Rory sat on the Devil's Steps at Rotherhithe. Below them, a seething, sullen Thames slapped against the river wall, as if it was trying to punish it. The river was choked with boats and barges, and although it was another sweltering day, a smoggy yellow haze lay over the city, and the smell from both the river and the nearby tannery was unpleasantly pungent. The girls were hot and tired after a fruitless afternoon spent knocking on the doors of lodging houses looking for Amy.

The day before, they had gone with the inspector and several policemen to Rotherhithe and shown the inspector the alleyway where they had dropped Amy off on the night the Doomstone was stolen. The police visited all the houses in the vicinity, but they had found no trace of anybody answering to either Amy's name or description. The inspector seemed much more interested in Jem. But Rose found it difficult to believe that Jem – easily led, betting-mad, but essentially sweet-natured – was responsible for the crime of the century. She wasn't at all convinced that quiet little Amy was responsible either, although her vanishing act seemed to suggest otherwise.

"It's as if she's disappeared off the face of the earth," said Rory, unbuttoning her new boots – handmade by the look of them – to allow the air to get to her stockinged feet.

"The question is, why?" asked Rose.

"Maybe she thought the inspector was going to arrest her for stealing the Doomstone," said Effie.

"Or maybe she was just unhappy and wanted to get away from Lydia," said Aurora.

Rose examined her friend beadily. "Is Lydia unkind to her?"

"Not exactly unkind. Just dismissive and demanding." She paused. "She is always delightful to Amy in front of Edward, but when he's not around she sometimes loses her temper, and tells Amy that she's stupid and knows nothing." Rory spoke fiercely and looked straight ahead, not meeting Rose's eye. Rose wondered whether Lydia's unkindness extended to Rory when her father was not around.

"That's how the rich behave to the poor," said Effie gloomily. "Me mum always said never to go into service; they buy your labour but they want to own you body an' soul."

"Rory, have you told your father about how Lydia behaves towards Amy?" asked Rose.

"There's no point," said Aurora gruffly. "Lydia can do no wrong in his eyes."

"Maybe you should open them for him?"

Aurora sighed. "It's hard, Rosie. Edward and I are still getting to know each other. Sometimes he still feels more like a stranger to me than my father. I know he's fond of me and I am of him. But we still don't really know each other like a father and daughter who have known each other since the day a child is born. Sometimes I see him looking at me, and I wonder if he's thinking whether there must have been a terrible mistake, and I'm not really his daughter."

"Oh, Rory," said Rose, squeezing Aurora's

hand. "I've seen Edward looking at you too, and it's with wonder – wonder that he's found the daughter who he thought was dead. And there can be no doubt that you are father and daughter – you are like two peas in a pod." But she thought how hard it must be for Aurora. Everyone said that her story was like a fairy tale. But, thought Rose darkly, fairy tales always just ended abruptly with "they lived happily ever after" and it was much harder to negotiate and navigate a real-life happy ever after.

Rose stood up. "Shall we carry on?"

"Rosie, my feet are killing me," said Aurora, "and I said I'd meet Edward at the Pall Mall at five. Why don't you come? You can see *Hamlet* again with me. We're wasting our time here. The police have already gone door to door, and if they couldn't find Amy, why should we do any better? She's obviously lied about where she was living, has covered her tracks and doesn't want to be found. Maybe she did steal the Doomstone and she's fled with it."

Rose was tempted to go with Rory. But she shook her head and looked at Effie, who was apologetic.

"I can't stay much longer either, Rosie. I've

got to get back to Campion's. I promised Mr Gandini I'd rehearse the new act with him."

"What is it?" asked Rory curiously. Effie put a finger to her mouth to indicate her lips were sealed.

"But it's going to be a real crowd-pleaser when it's ready, which won't be for a few days. If we can get it right, Thomas will have to extend Campion's to meet the demand for tickets. Mr Gandini's that confident about it."

"Effie," asked Rose, "why do you always call Gandini *Mr* Gandini? Nobody else does."

"He deserves it," said Effie. "He's a real gent in every way. I really like him. He's kind."

Rose smiled, but her heart stuttered. Gandini wouldn't stay at Campion's forever. He would move on. Would Effie move on with him? Rose realised that she might be going to lose both Rory and Effie very soon. She'd be on her own again at Campion's. The thought of them abandoning her made her forlorn.

"Well, I'm going to try a few more houses," said Rose. "I'll be back at Campion's in time to see the Illustrious Gandini, the Great Wizard of the North, and his very charming assist—" She suddenly broke off.

"That's it!" she said. "I knew something wasn't quite right, the night we first met Lydia and Amy."

"What weren't right? Spit it out, Rosie."

"Do you remember? We'd all gone down to the cabs ready to set off from the Pall Mall for Campion's. We were just about to leave when Amy came rushing out."

"Yes, Lydia had forgotten her," said Effie, "an' offered her a lift to her lodgings in Rotherhithe." She suddenly looked excited. "She said it were by the river. But where we dropped her, and where the police were looking, was way back from here."

"That's right," said Rose. "That's clever of you, Effie. I had forgotten that. But there's something more."

Rory wrinkled her forehead, thinking. "Lydia suggested that Amy came with us all to Campion's."

"And what did Amy say?"

The others shrugged.

"I dunno," said Effie. "Yes, please?"

Rose looked triumphant. "She said that she would like to come and see the Illustrious Gandini."

Rory and Effie shrugged. "Why's that significant?"

"Because nobody had mentioned Gandini, so how did she know he was performing?"

The others looked sceptical.

"Maybe she'd heard he was on the bill. Maybe she'd seen a poster? Maybe you misremembered – it was ages ago."

"Perhaps, but I remembered thinking there was something odd at the time but I couldn't quite put my finger on it. Listen, you go back. I'll ask around a bit more, at the lodgings close to the river."

* ✷ *

Rose retraced her steps along the riverfront. She was too hot and she had found no trace of Amy. It was as if the girl had simply vanished, like a magician's assistant in a conjuring act. She had tried all the houses with signs saying that they took lodgers along the riverfront, and she was walking in the direction of Campion's. She had been silly to think that she could do better than the police. But she was worried about Amy. What if she had been beaten up like Jem? What if she had escaped with the Doomstone, and Jem, if he recovered, was going to end up taking the blame?

She walked past a small house. It was down at heel but the windows were clean, even if the shutters were in need of a lick of paint. There was no sign suggesting that the house took lodgers, but something caught her eye through the glass. A china duck sitting forlornly on the windowsill next to a pile of pebbles and shells, perhaps dusty mementoes of a long-ago seaside trip. It reminded her of how Amy had come alive when she had been talking about visiting Southend. Maybe she had come here, seen the display in the window and found lodgings here. It was worth a try.

Rose lifted the knocker and let it fall. A moment passed and then she heard footsteps and a woman's weary voice telling a child to let go of her skirts. The door was pulled open and an exhausted-looking woman wearing an apron stood before her, tucking a wayward strand of hair into her cap with one hand while trying to soothe the infant over her shoulder with another. Two toddlers, obviously twins, peeped shyly from behind her skirts, one trailing a wooden soldier, the other a frayed blanket. The woman looked at Rose expectantly.

"I've come to see my sister. I've heard she's lodging here. Amy."

The woman shook her head. "There's no Amy here. You've got the wrong place."

"But you do take lodgers?" The woman nodded. "Maybe she's calling herself something else. She looks about my age. But she's younger. Reddish-gold hair, gooseberry-green eyes. Lanky. She's got a mustard-yellow dress," said Rose quickly.

The woman nodded. "Oh, you mean Melly. Least, that's what she called herself. I don't asks no questions, as long as them's respectable, eats what I give 'em and pays the rent up front and don't want too much hot water. I had one girl wanted a hot bath every week." The woman looked outraged. "But Melly's been easy enough. Keeps herself to herself. Shy little thing." She peered more closely at Rose.

"You don't look much alike for sisters."

"I take after the other side of the family," said Rose quickly. "Can I speak to Amy – er, Melly?"

The woman shook her head. "We'd all like to speak to her. Me included. Haven't seen her for two days. She owes rent. I've known them skip before. They try and do a moonlight flit but they don't realise I sleep with one ear open."

"So she's gone?" asked Rose.

"So it seems, but your sister ain't like the others. She's gone, but she's not taken nothing with her. Not that she had much to take."

Rose frowned. "Didn't you think that something might have happened to her, something bad?"

The woman sighed. "Of course it crossed my mind. But it's none of my business what the lodgers gets up to, as long as they pays their rent and don't bring trouble knocking on my door. If they want to call themselves Amy or Melly or whatever, I'm easy. I've got enough to cope with keeping body and soul together since my Mick lost a leg down on the docks."

"I'm sorry about your husband," said Rose, "but I'm worried about Amy, I mean Melly. She's missing. She hasn't been seen at work either. It's not like her."

The woman looked guilty. "I don't want you thinking I've got a heart of stone. It's been hanging heavy on me. There's summat not right. I was going to report it to the police if she didn't come back tonight." She sighed. "I like Melly. She's good with the kiddies too. Sometimes she does magic tricks for them. Makes that sparkling blue bauble she's got disappear in front of your eyes."

Rose's eyes widened and she coughed to disguise her surprise, but the woman didn't notice.

"Blue bauble?"

"Yes, lovely sparkling thing. She said it was a Christmas tree decoration, pretty but worthless. My Mick said she could have done a magic act in one of them halls. Right little magician, she is."

"Can I see her room?" asked Rose, trying to suppress her excitement.

The woman hesitated. "What if she comes back and I've been letting you rummage through her things?"

"Just a quick peek," said Rose. "I'm her sister, I might notice if something is amiss." She took some coins out of her pocket and held them out in her palm. "I could pay the rent she owes so you're not out of pocket."

A man's feeble voice could be heard calling: "Lorrie! What's keeping you, Lorrie?"

The woman glanced back with a worried frown, as one of the twins set up a wail and the baby began to bawl.

"Don't think me heartless," she said, "but we've all got to live." And she scooped the coins out of Rose's palm and nodded up the narrow stairs.

"Two flights up, then the door on the left. It's not locked. Not that you'll find much. I poked my head in and it's neat as a pin, just as it always was. Couldn't see the bauble, mind, and that often sat on the top of the chest of drawers. Call when you're leaving."

Rose stepped inside Amy's room. The woman was right – Amy didn't have much to her name. There was something about the room that reminded Rose of a stage set, as if it was a space that had been carefully arranged and was holding its breath waiting for something to happen. It was scrupulously neat. Nothing was out of place. Two dresses hung forlornly from a rail next to a coat, good quality but worn. The mustard-yellow dress was missing. In a drawer she found some neatly folded undergarments. She pulled up the cheap paper that had been used to line the drawer. Underneath was a copy of *The Times*, with the front-page story telling of the night at Campion's when the

Doomstone went missing and rehashing the story of the curse. The bit about the curse had been underlined in thick black ink. It was the only thing that connected Amy, or Melly, to the room at all. It was as if she hadn't lived here but had merely existed. Rose saw the corner of something that had slipped down the back of the drawer. She pulled it out. It was a seaside scene of little fishermen's cottages drawn in charcoal.

The small, narrow bed was neatly made. A wooden doll sat propped up on the pillow. There was something about the doll, with her out-of-proportion legs and green eyes, that Rose found heart-breaking, as if what she was looking at was Amy herself. She picked up the doll and underneath there was a small folded piece of paper. She unfolded the paper. There were just a few lines written in blue ink.

"Forgive me for causing such trouble. There is nobody to miss me. I am all alone in the world. I made a mistake and I can't live with myself. I stole the Doomstone. Chance gave me the opportunity and the means, and I gave in to temptation on a whim, but it has been the doom of me. I cannot eat and I dare not go to sleep. I cannot go on. I'm cursed. The Doomstone is an evil thing. All I can do to atone for my crime is to rid the world of both it and myself. May God forgive me my sins. Amy."

Rose put her hand over her mouth and tears filled her eyes. She rushed down the stairs shouting, "Missus! Missus!" The woman looked up with anxious eyes.

"We must fetch the police," said Rose, and she held out the note to the woman. "Something terrible has happened to Amy."

15

Everyone was gathering in Campion's auditorium waiting for the inspector to arrive. The mood was sombre. Rose found she couldn't settle to anything. She was too upset thinking about poor Amy. She picked up some props at the side of the stage and decided to busy herself by taking them back to the prop store. She neared the door and paused, hearing voices. It was Lydia and Stratford-Mark. In his low voice, the latter was saying:

"Don't you forget, I'm keeping a close eye on you, Lydia. I've made you and I can break you. I know all about you. We made a deal and feelings can't be allowed to get in the way of it."

The door to the dressing room opposite the prop store was ajar and Rose was tempted to slip inside, but she hardly dared breathe, let alone move, as Lydia said:

"Don't threaten me, Stratford-Mark, or I may just snap in half to spite you. Haven't I been as good as my word so far? Even though I fervently wish I had never agreed to our arrangement in the first place. We have to trust each other. We have no choice. But I warn you – if you push me too far, it will be the worse for both of us. We will both lose everything."

Someone moved towards the prop room door, and Rose took a step backwards into the dressing room, standing behind the door and peering through the crack as Lydia swept out of the prop store towards the stage, followed by a scowling Stratford-Mark hobbling to keep up like a wounded bull. Rose took a deep breath. Her head was spinning with what she had heard. What was the deal that Lydia and Stratford-Mark had made? She was suddenly aware she was not alone in the room. She spun round. Billy Proctor was standing further back in the room.

"What are you doing here?" she asked indignantly.

Billy gave a little smirk. "Apparently, exactly the same thing as you, Rose Campion.

Eavesdropping on other people's private conversations." He strolled away, leaving Rose feeling a mixture of fury and shame.

* ✱ *

Inspector Cliff peered around at everyone gathered in the auditorium. His eyes were serious. Everyone from Campion's was there, but Stratford-Mark had left shortly before the meeting began. Lydia was clinging to Edward's arm, pale and nervous. Edward's distress was all too evident. Gandini was standing behind them, drumming his fingers on the wall. Billy Proctor was slouching against one of the pillars with a studied nonchalance. He saw Rose looking at him and averted his gaze, as if he didn't want to make eye contact. Everyone knew by now what Rose had discovered at Amy's lodgings, although she had confessed only to Effie and Aurora and the inspector how she had employed deception, pretending to be Amy's sister, to gain access to her room.

"Ladies and gentlemen, thank you for coming. I wanted to inform you about the latest developments in the investigation into the theft of the Star of the Sea. I know that you are all aware by now of the disappearance of

Miss Duchamps's dresser, Amy, as she was calling herself, and the note that was found by Rose Campion suggesting that Amy had taken her own life. It seems that Amy was an alias – possibly one of several that the girl was using. The references with which she supplied Miss Duchamps were false. Amy was clearly not all that she seemed, and we may never find out exactly who she really was."

Lydia put her hand to her mouth, and her eyes were wide with shock. "Amy lied to me? What a trusting fool I was to be taken in by her! She tried to slit my throat when she stole the Doomstone. I would never have believed it of her. She seemed such a quiet girl, and quieter still in recent days – as if something was troubling her."

The inspector continued. "We have made inquiries but so far we have discovered nothing about the girl, or who she was and where she came from. However, we have discovered some evidence that strongly indicates Amy did indeed throw herself into the Thames with the Doomstone, to her death. We cannot be sure of that scenario but we do have two witnesses who have said that they both saw a girl in a mustard dress down by the Devil's Steps in Rotherhithe very late on the night in question. One of those witnesses, on his way home from the Anchor Inn, has said that he thinks the girl might have been in some distress."

Lydia was dabbing at her eyes. Rose's throat was raw and she swallowed hard.

"We have not as yet recovered a body but we hope to do so. What goes into the Thames doesn't always come out again, and if it does it can sometimes be weeks or months later. But we have every reason to believe that Amy did indeed throw herself into the river. One of the clues we have is the yellow dress. It was discovered by mudlarks on the Devil's Steps at Rotherhithe on the night she disappeared, and sold on to a local market stall. The dress was still on the stall."

He suddenly produced the dress from out of the box in front of him, just as a magician produces a rabbit out of a hat, in what Rose thought was a curiously calculated theatrical gesture. If it was, it had the desired effect. There were audible gasps. Edward gulped in astonishment. Gandini closed his eyes as if in pain. Lydia gave a little squeal. Thomas passed his hand despairingly across his forehead. It was as if poor Amy was here in the room with them, her absence magnified to unbearable proportions by the mustard-coloured garment that they had all seen her wearing, both on the night of the disappearance of the Doomstone and often since.

The inspector paused again, as if letting them all consider the significance of the dress. Then he said, "I can also confirm that the note discovered in Amy's lodging house matches samples of Amy's handwriting that Miss Duchamps gave us. My men and I have considered the evidence carefully and we believe that Amy was indeed responsible for the theft of the Doomstone. We fear that both Amy and the diamond are somewhere at the bottom of the Thames and may never be recovered."

"The curse caught up with her!" blurted Effie. "Poor little Amy was doomed as soon as she stole that diamond. Her fate was sealed." She saw everyone looking at her and turned scarlet.

"In the circumstances," continued the inspector, "we are bringing the inquiry into the disappearance of the Star of the Sea to an end. So I am here to tell you that I will be returning to

Scotland Yard to announce that the case is now closed."

There was a buzz of excitement as everyone began talking at once. Rose saw Billy Proctor give a little smile that seemed to suggest some secret satisfaction or knowledge. Gandini was frowning slightly, as if he was thinking hard, and his gaze was moody. Edward seemed distracted. Lydia was the centre of several people's attention as she explained that of course she was broken-hearted at dear little Amy's demise, and only wished she could have done something to save the girl from herself, but now she thought about it, the girl had always been extremely evasive about where she came from, and although she, Lydia, would never speak ill of the dead, there had been something low and cunning about Amy. She placed her hand on the inspector's arm and looked at him with her big eyes.

"We have much to thank you for, Inspector."

The inspector gave a curt little bow. "There was little to solve. Once we found out about the girl's suicide, it was pretty well an open-and-shut case." He nodded to Thomas. "I must get back to the Yard."

He walked towards the stage door. Rose

watched him go, a scowl on her face. She couldn't believe it! The police were closing the case with so many unanswered questions. She hesitated and then she ran after him. The inspector was at the far end of the yard with his hand already on the gate.

"Inspector Cliff," she called.

He turned round and smiled kindly as she approached. "Rose. You knew Amy and you discovered the note; this must be hard for you. If there's anything I can do…"

"Well, actually you can," said Rose bluntly. "I just want to know if it's common for people who commit suicide to remove their clothes before jumping in the river. The bodies of people who've thrown themselves in are regularly fished out around here, and unless they've been in there for weeks, they're always fully clothed."

There was a tiny electric pause, and then the inspector said levelly, "It's uncommon but not unheard of for those intent on self-harm to remove their clothing." He looked hard at Rose. "Don't think that we didn't consider the fact that Amy had removed her dress before she entered the water." He seemed to be looking beyond Rose when he said, in a voice that carried, "The case is closed. We are quite confident our deliberations are correct, and we have other pressing cases to attend to at Scotland Yard." Then, in a much lowered voice, he said, "Keep safe, Rose, and leave the detecting to the detectives." Then he was gone.

Rose turned back towards Campion's. Edward, Lydia, Billy and Gandini were all standing by the stage door watching her. It made Rose feel uncomfortable. She gave them an awkward little smile and went inside.

"Where've you been, Rose?" asked Aurora.

"I was talking to the inspector."

"It's so awful about Amy," said Effie. "I don't know how anyone could take their own life like that. However bad things got."

"I don't think she did," said Rose. She gathered the others closer and then she whispered, "I think Amy was murdered. And I'm going to try to prove it."

16

"That's perfect," said Rose, taking the picture that Effie had drawn on a sketchpad and examining it closely.

"You are clever, Effie. You've caught Billy Proctor's likeness exactly. It's as good as one of those photographs."

Rose was on a mission. She had decided that Billy Proctor needed urgent investigation. If Amy had been murdered, as she believed, and her death was connected with the theft of the Doomstone, she was increasingly certain that Billy was the culprit. She had tried to raise her suspicions with Thomas, but he would not be persuaded even when she had told him that she was quite sure that she had spotted Billy at Holloway Prison, and was certain he was going to visit the underworld mastermind known as the Duchess.

"You are putting two and two together and making five, Rosie," said Thomas patiently. "You are not even one hundred per cent certain it was Billy you saw outside the prison, and even if it was, he might just have been passing and it could have been a coincidence."

"But Julia Devonish said the Duchess was having a visitor. I think it was Billy and that's why he was at Holloway."

Thomas was not convinced. "Even if he was visiting this so-called Duchess, it doesn't make him a criminal by association. Listen, Rose, I know you don't like Billy much, and with reason – he does seem particularly surly with you – but gracelessness is not a crime, and although he may have lied to me about his experience as a barman, he is learning and getting better." He peered at Rose intently. "Don't tell me that you've never told a lie when you've felt the need."

Rose couldn't help blushing. She had told quite a few recently. She covered her discomfort by demanding, "Did you even check his references?"

Now it was Thomas's turn to look bashful and he shook his head. "No. But I seldom do, Rosie. Gut instinct has always stood me in good stead, and gut instinct told me that, for all his failings, at heart Billy is a decent sort."

Rose had come away from the conversation determined to look further into Billy's background, which was why they were outside the Anchor in Rotherhithe.

"Come on, let's go in," she said to Effie. They stood up and walked to the door and went inside. The place fell silent and the few men sitting on stools at wooden tables turned to stare at them. They didn't look friendly. Effie faltered, but Rose marched across the sawdust-covered floor to the bar, where a surly-looking man was spitting on greasy glasses to clean them.

"What do you two want?" he grunted. Rose held out the charcoal drawing of Billy Proctor. It really was very good: Effie had pinned the discontented expression in Billy Proctor's eyes on the paper.

"Do you know this man?"

The barman's eyes flicked over the drawing. "Who's asking?"

"He's working for my da. As a barman. He

had a reference from here."

The barman snorted. Rose noticed that one of the customers, a stooped man, thin as a pencil, sitting at a corner table, was gazing at them with interest.

"He did, did he? Well, it was forged. Never set eyes on him in me life and I've bin the landlord here for ten years past."

"Ah, well, that explains why he's so bad at his job. If you had trained him I'm sure he would be more than competent," said Rose, trying to keep her tone sincere. Billy Proctor may be inefficient, but at least nobody had ever spotted him spitting on the glasses to clean them.

"Look, if you've got what you want to know, get out. We've had the Blues buzzing around and enough questions being asked since that girl topped herself in the river. Too many questions is never good for business, an' I don't know why they're so interested. What's one more child in the river? What was special 'bout that one?"

"I understand you don't want trouble," said Rose sympathetically. "But there is one thing more you could help us with and it concerns the girl. There was a witness, someone who had been drinking here on the night she died, who

184

told the police he'd seen her standing on the Devil's Steps looking distressed. I'd like to talk to him. The thing is, the girl ... the girl who died ... she was my sister. I just want to know what happened. The police could tell us so little."

The landlord had the grace to look shamed. But he still spoke stonily. "Sorry. I can't help you. Time you two were moving on. You're clogging up the place."

"We're sorry to have bothered you," said Rose politely, although inside she was certain that the shifty landlord knew more than he was letting on. She and Effie walked back out on to the riverside path with as much dignity as they could muster. Once they were safely beyond hearing, Effie said, "Rose Campion, you are such a fibber. Going round telling people that you were poor Amy's sister. It's outrageous. You're so good I almost believed you meself."

Rose blushed, and said defensively, "It's not proper lies. I'm only doing it to try and find out what happened to poor Amy."

"I know," said Effie, "but I do think—"

There was a low whistle behind them. They turned and the thin, stooped man who had been sitting in the corner of the Anchor was standing on the path. He limped towards them and indicated they should move away from the river path and down one of the alleyways between the houses, where he followed them.

"It was me," he said gruffly, a hint of nerves in his voice. "I told the Blues I'd seen yer sister on the Devil's Steps."

Rose smiled gently at the man. "Thank you for talking to us. I'm really grateful. It's just that the police have so little information about what happened to poor Amy."

The man looked at Rose with faded cornflower eyes. "My sister," said the man, "she died off the very same steps, fifty year ago. She had a smile as sweet as honey. They say she did herself in like your sister. But I dunno. She had got in with a bad crowd."

"I'm so sorry," said Rose softly, feeling intensely guilty that she was pretending to be Amy's bereaved sister. "Are you saying that you think your sister might have been murdered?"

The man shrugged. "I dunno what to think. It's too long ago to rake it over, but I saw your sister in the mustard dress that night."

"Did you speak to her?" The man shook his

head. "But you told the police that she seemed distressed?"

The man's nerves resurfaced. "Yeah, but she weren't alone," he mumbled.

"Who was with her? Man or woman?"

"Man."

"Did you tell the police this?"

The man shook his head. "I didn't want to get too involved. Bod, the landlord from the Anchor, told us all to keep our mouths shut when the Blues came round. Say as little as possible. He's worried. He runs a gambling den in the basement. Not just cards, though there's plenty of that, but illegal stuff: cockfighting, dog-fighting, and the like. So I jest told the Blues I'd seen her on the steps, which I did. It was only when you came into the pub and talked about her being your sister that I thought about me own loss and how if some'un had seen me sister on the night she died I'd like to have talked to them. Your sister, she was upset. She was telling the man to go away, that she didn't want to talk to him. I thought maybe it was a pa talking to his wayward daughter. I didn't see your sister's face, she had her back to me, just saw the mustard dress."

"Would you recognise the man if you saw him again?" asked Rose.

"I dunno. It was dark."

Rose indicated to Effie to show her sketch of Billy Proctor to the man. The man looked and shook his head.

"Nah, never seen him before. Weren't him."

Rose nodded. So the landlord had been telling the truth about not knowing about Billy Proctor, and Billy had definitely lied about working at the Anchor. Effie went to close her pad, and as she did so a loose page fell to the ground. It was the one on which she had sketched the faces of those sitting outside Campion's in the yard on that balmy night a couple of weeks previously, when they had all been eating penny licks. Rose picked it up and went to pass it to Effie, and as she did so, the man stopped her and pointed to a face on the page.

"I know this one. Him's Jem – he's always hanging around the Anchor when there's a gambling session. They say he has the luck of the devil when it comes to the cards. Not that the luck of the devil makes you popular, mind. Some says he's a cheat, but if he is, nobody knows how he does it."

Rose's heart sank. "Was he at the Anchor on the night that Amy died?"

The man nodded. "I think summat happened with him too. But I don't know what. Best to turn a blind eye to what goes on downstairs."

"Do you think that he could have been the man you saw with Amy that night?"

The man shook his head. "He were at the Anchor for sure, but no, it weren't him I saw on the steps. But if I was a betting man, I'd say it was this one," he said stabbing his finger. "This is the one who I saw with your sister."

Rose and Effie starred at each other in shock. The picture that the man's gnarled finger was pointing at was of Aurora's father, Edward, Lord Easingford.

17

Rose turned the corner and walked down the side of the Pall Mall Theatre towards the stage door. She was going to join Aurora at the theatre to watch a rehearsal of *Macbeth*, which was opening the following week. She was looking forward to seeing Aurora, who had been at Silver Square with Edward for the last three nights. But she was apprehensive too. Aurora had sent a note the previous evening to say that she couldn't return to Campion's as expected. Her absence meant they had to take the bicycle act off the bill, which had made Rose fret again that Aurora was growing away from her and Campion's.

Effie had seen Rose's frown when she had read the note sent by Aurora, and she said quietly, "You've got to let her go, Rosie, if that's what she wants. Poor Ror's caught between two worlds. It's eating her up. I can see it in her face. She doesn't know whether she's one of us or one of them toffs. She's got to find out for herself which she wants to be, or find a comfortable way to move easily between the two. If you try and force her to choose between being a lady and Campion's you'll drive her away for sure. Be patient with her."

Rose knew that wise little Effie was right, but it didn't stop her feeling as if she, Thomas, Effie and her beloved Campion's had somehow been judged and found wanting by Aurora. Maybe by Edward too, particularly now that he was deeply involved with Lydia, with all her airs and graces. Then there was the issue of Edward being spotted on the Devil's Steps at Rotherhithe with Amy on the night of her death. She and Effie had discussed it at length.

"Look, Rosie," said Effie. "I can't believe our Eddie would have anything to do with anything bad."

"But what was he doing at Rotherhithe with Amy on the night she died?"

"Well, not murdering her, of that I'm sure. If

he was there at all," she added darkly. "Maybe that bloke from the Anchor was mistaken. Rosie, I know you reckon that poor Amy was done away with, but don't you think you're getting a bit ahead of yourself? If the inspector thinks she drowned herself maybe he's got good reason. Let it go."

"But there's something else," said Rose. "Edward lied to Lydia the night Amy died. I heard him tell her he had business with Thomas, but he didn't. Thomas went straight to bed. Amy left Campion's almost as soon as the hansom had left with Lydia, and I saw Edward leave shortly after. Maybe he followed Amy."

"Maybe he did and maybe he didn't," said Effie, "and maybe if he did he's already told the inspector. Listen, Rosie, leave it to the police."

Rose had nodded reluctantly but she felt like a terrier with a bone that she couldn't let go of.

She dawdled for a moment by a shop, trying to delay the moment when she faced Aurora, in case her friend was going to tell her that their days as a double act were over. She glanced towards the stage door and to her surprise she saw Gandini leaving. She almost called out to him, but she saw his grim face and hesitated, and he didn't even notice her as he strode by on the opposite side of the road. She watched his retreating back and wondered who he had been visiting at the Pall Mall.

She was about to cross the road when she saw another man come out of the stage door. It was the man with the handlebar moustache wearing the peacock-blue waistcoat who had spoken to her and the others at the Pall Mall on the night of Edward's debut as Hamlet, and told them all about Lydia and the Doomstone. He had also been at Campion's when the Doomstone went missing, and then again when she had seen him exchanging a nod with Edward, before he disappeared without a trace. Once again he was dressed less flamboyantly today, in a dark suit and silk top hat, but with a telltale vivid flash of blue in his tie and handkerchief. The man turned the corner and was heading up towards Piccadilly. Rose pulled her hat down over her face, relieved she was wearing one, and set off in pursuit.

At Piccadilly the man waited to cross the street and then entered a commanding building. It was a bank. Rose smoothed her gloves, thankful that her determination not to show Aurora up in any way had made her put them on, adjusted her hat and walked briskly towards the door. A doorman opened it for her, and although she didn't feel at all confident, she sailed through as if she was always going into banks. The man from the Pall Mall was talking to another very smart man in a tailcoat, who Rose guessed might be the manager of the bank. Rose moved behind a pillar and watched them.

"Can I help you, madam?" said a voice. A snooty-looking clerk peered down at her as if doubting her right to be in the building. Rose tried not to feel intimidated.

"I think I was supposed to meet my father here," she said in her poshest voice. "But maybe I was mistaken. Perhaps he meant for me to meet him at Coutts."

"On the Strand, madam," said the man.

"Of course," said Rose. "How silly of me. But tell me, who is that gentleman over there? He looks very familiar."

The man glanced over. "That is Mr Augustus Drover, madam. One of our best customers."

"I think he's a friend of my father's," said Rose.

"Does your father trade in diamonds?" asked the man.

Rose shook her head and said innocently, "Is that Mr Drover's business? I must be mistaken then. My father is in shipping." The lie fell off her tongue so easily that she felt quite queasy about the way she had developed such a facility for deceit. But she added, "Diamonds! How exciting."

"Indeed, madam. To think that some of the most flawless gemstones in the world have passed through his hands. He is one of our most valued customers."

"I mustn't keep you. I ought to go and find my father. Thank you for your help," said Rose sweetly, and she left the bank. Outside, her heart beating very fast, she set off back to the Pall Mall. She slipped through the stage door and said hello to Grumbles, the stage-doorkeeper.

"I saw Mr Gandini leaving."

Grumbles grunted and nodded. "'im supposed to be a wizard but he don't ever seem to be able to magic me up a tip."

"So he's been before?" asked Rose.

"Yes, to see Miss Duchamps, and today she looked most put out to see 'im."

"There was another man here, he left about ten minutes ago. Handlebar moustache, wearing a top hat and dark suit with pinstripe trousers. His name was Mr Drover," said Rose urgently.

"Oh, 'im," said Grumbles grumpily. "He walked all over me freshly washed floor."

"Who did he come to see?"

"His Lordship. He came to see young Edward."

Rose's heart sank to her boots.

18

"What's the matter, Rosie?" asked Aurora, who was dressed in the sapphire silk tea gown. Her hair had been curled. "There's something bothering you." They were sitting together on the chaise longue in Edward's dressing room, but there was an awkwardness between them. Edward had gone out to see his tailor.

"It's nothing," said Rose, but she couldn't quite meet Aurora's eye. Her mind was working furiously. Could Edward really have had something to do with the disappearance of the Doomstone? Or, if not its initial disappearance, with whatever had happened to it subsequently? It was ludicrous to even contemplate such a thing. Why on earth would Edward, who already had money, position and success, risk it all? But surely it was too much of a coincidence that two men who had both been present the night the Doomstone was stolen were meeting together so soon after the mysterious disappearance of Amy. Could they be involved in her murder? Could Edward be implicated in something so foul?

"I've got something to tell you, Rose," said Aurora, standing up and putting some distance between the two of them. Rose stiffened at Aurora's use of Rose rather than Rosie. "Things have changed. I've got to think of the future. We're growing up. I want to stop doing the bicycle act. It's just not right for someone in my position. It's not befitting any more."

Rose's throat constricted and her eyes felt gritty. The effort to stop herself from crying meant that her words were spat out, making her sound angry when she only felt hurt and sad.

"What do you mean – 'befitting'?" she said. "Why is it befitting for me and not for you?"

Aurora sighed. "Don't make this hard for me, Rosie. You know why. It's because of my change in circumstances."

"Have you talked to Edward about this? Does he think that performing in a music hall is unbefitting for his daughter?" asked Rose, rising to her feet, and again the pain in her heart made the word "befitting" come out with a snarl.

Aurora shook her head helplessly. "No, I haven't spoken to him. But people whisper. You know they do, whispering about the lord's daughter who performs on a music-hall stage."

"Ignore them, they're just narrow-minded, stuck-up cows. Why do you want their approval? They're not worth it. Anyway, Edward performs on stage too," said Rose.

"It's not at all the same," said Aurora. "It may be unusual for a lord to be on stage playing Hamlet, but it's the legitimate theatre. The Pall Mall attracts audiences from the cream of society. Lydia says it's not the same as me dressing up as a boy to be gawped at by all and sundry."

Rose gave a snort. "Gawped at by all and sundry? Oh, Rory, I didn't know you had turned into such a little snob."

"Don't be unfair, Rose," said Aurora. "I can't help who I am. I never asked to be born the daughter of a lord. I can't help that I'm a lady now, and have to behave like one. I'm sorry, but that's the way it is. I won't be performing the bicycle act any more. Maybe you could ask

Effie, now she's got a taste for being on stage. She'd be good at it."

Rose was so distraught she didn't notice the crack in Aurora's voice.

"Good at it because she's not a lady and nobody could ever mistake her for one, I suppose!" said Rose sarcastically. "I had no idea, Miss High and Mighty Lady Aurora, that you have been looking down your nose at us all this time."

"I haven't," wailed Aurora. "It's just I feel as if I'm being torn apart. It's not just the toffs who whisper. When I'm at Campion's, people talk too. They treat me differently, as if I'm not quite one of them any more. Edward doesn't notice, but I do because I know what it was like before, when I was just Aurora Scarletti, the Infant Phenomenon." She sighed. "This is going to sound terrible, but sometimes I wish I could turn back the clock. Sometimes I wish that it was you who had turned out to be Edward's daughter and not me. Sometimes I just want everything to go back to how it was before I discovered I was the daughter of a lord, when you and I were first friends and we were working on the bicycle act together." Her eyes welled tears.

Rose gave a sad little smile. "There have been

times when I envied you having found your real father, and knowing who you really are, rather than being a nobody like me, abandoned on a doorstep with no history, not even a name. Oh, Rory, I'm sorry," said Rose, flinging her arms around Aurora. "I know it must be difficult for you. I don't really think you're a snob. I don't know why I said it. I was hurt that you want to give up the bicycle act. It won't be the same without you. Maybe I'll retire it – I don't want to do it with anyone else, not even Effie."

"I wish it could be different," whispered Aurora tearfully.

The two stood in silence for a moment.

Then Aurora asked, "There's something else bothering you, Rosie, isn't there? Did something happen that you're not telling me about?"

"It doesn't matter," said Rose, twisting one of Rory's rusty-brown curls through her fingers. She wasn't going to risk upsetting Aurora by voicing her suspicions about Edward, the diamond merchant and the Doomstone.

"Go on, tell," insisted Aurora.

Rose hesitated. She decided not to mention the man from the Anchor seeing Edward with Amy on the night she died. After all, it would sound as if she was accusing Edward of murder. But she quickly explained about seeing the man leaving the Pall Mall, following him to the bank and discovering he was a renowned diamond merchant.

"But why are you concerned about that?" asked Aurora with a frown.

Rose took a deep breath. "Because when I asked Grumbles at the stage door, the person the diamond merchant had come to see was … was … Edward."

For a second Aurora looked at Rose, her face white with shock.

"I know," stuttered Rose. "It's just too silly to think that Edward could have had anything to do with the disappearance of the Doomstone."

Two high spots of colour appeared on Aurora's cheeks. "And that's what you think, Rose?" Her voice was so steely and cold it made Rose feel as if a deep well had opened up inside her. "You think that my father is a thief?"

"I don't know what to think," she whispered.

Aurora eyes blazed. "Everyone always says that you're so clever, Rose Campion. But I think you are a blind fool who thinks she knows better than everyone else, even the police, and who is trying to play detective when everyone, even Inspector Cliff, is convinced that Amy stole the Doomstone and it's at the bottom of the Thames with her. But will you listen? No, because you think you are cleverer than everyone else, and go round telling all sorts of lies to get information, and making wild accusations without any real evidence. You disgust me, Rose."

"I'm not saying that Edward had anything to do with the disappearance of the Doomstone," protested Rose desperately.

"But that's what you think, isn't it? You think he's trying to dispose of it. How could you, Rose! When he's been so kind and generous to Thomas, lending him money when he desperately needed it. How could you even think that my father might be involved in something shady? Is that what you really think of him, even when he's been so kind to you, encouraging you in your acting? Is this how you repay him? By thinking the very worst of him?"

"I don't know what to think," whispered Rose. "All I know is that Mr Drover had a meeting with Edward, and I thought it was strange, given Mr Drover's profession and the fact that he was present at Campion's on the night of the disappearance of the Doomstone."

"Well, I don't know why Mr Drover was at Campion's that night. Diamond merchants have as much right to go to the music hall to see a magic act as anyone else. It's hardly suspicious behaviour. But I'll tell you exactly why Mr Drover was here at the theatre to see my father. He came to bring back one of the Easingford family diamonds that has been recut and reset to make a ring. An engagement ring. Edward has proposed to Lydia and she has accepted. They are to have a private marriage ceremony at St Olave's Church, the day after tomorrow at ten p.m. They are both keen to avoid any publicity. So Edward is not secretly disposing of the Doomstone that you seem to think he has stolen, he is simply marrying Lydia."

Aurora burst into noisy tears and Rose wasn't at all sure if she was now crying because she was so angry and outraged at Rose's accusation, or because Edward and Lydia were getting married.

"Oh, Rory, forgive me," said Rose, taking a step towards her friend.

Aurora put up her hands to stop her. "Don't you dare touch me, Rose Campion. I want nothing more to do with you. I know where all your nasty allegations come from: jealousy. You're just jealous that I've found my father, and now I'm getting a mother too. And you, you have neither."

Rose's eyes filled with tears. If Aurora had pierced her skin with a knife she couldn't have felt more pain. She remembered Aurora screaming at Lizzie Gawkin all those months ago when the truth of her birth had been discovered: "Rose Campion may not be my blood twin, but she will be my sister forever." To Rose it felt as if the bond between her and Aurora had been broken, and she didn't know how it could ever be repaired. She was such an idiot. She should have listened to Effie. The man from the Anchor must have made a mistake. All her suspicions were misplaced, and in her foolish attempt to play detective she had created a tear in her relationship with Rory that might never be mended.

19

Rose, Thomas and Edward had just taken their seats at a table near the front of Campion's auditorium. Gandini and Effie were unveiling their new act. Rose, Thomas and Edward had recently come from Thomas's office, which Effie was using as a dressing room. Edward had brought Effie flowers, a thoughtful gesture and one that had made Rose feel even more guilty about her suspicions of him. They chatted with Effie, who showed no sign of nerves, until she said that it was time for her to go downstairs and join Gandini in his dressing room.

"He says he finds it more soothing to have me with him just before a show," said Effie.

Lydia had given Effie an effusive kiss, wrapping her arms around her, and they had all set off downstairs together. Lydia had stopped to talk to the backstage hands, including Tobias, who as usual was very attentive.

Effie tripped off towards Gandini's dressing room with a big, confident smile on her face. Rose and Thomas grinned at each other to see Effie so self-assured and happy. She was transformed.

There was a mounting sense of excitement in the auditorium, which was packed to the rafters. It was as if the crowd sensed that something momentous was going to happen, even though there had been no formal announcement that tonight Gandini would be performing the notorious bullet catch. But somehow word seemed to have got around.

When Gandini had advised Thomas what he was planning, Thomas had expressed his concerns about the trick being performed at Campion's. Several stage magicians had died trying it, and Thomas didn't want blood on his hands.

"But, Thomas, Mr Gandini is a perfectionist," said Effie. "We've bin practising it for weeks. It's foolproof."

"If you had met as many idiots as I have over the years, you'd know that no trick's ever foolproof, Effie," said Thomas, shaking his head. "I don't like it at all. What if somebody gets injured?"

"They won't," said Gandini calmly. "The only person who could possibly get hurt is me, but if it makes you happier, perhaps on this first occasion that I perform the trick at Campion's I won't pick somebody completely at random to pull the trigger. Instead I'll choose somebody who I am certain is utterly trustworthy to point the gun and fire." He gazed at Thomas.

"You want me to do it?" said Thomas, looking thunderstruck. "I really don't think so. Even the thought makes my hand shake."

"Then I will ask Edward. I'm sure he will oblige. He is a trustworthy man. I have talked to him about the trick and its notorious history. He is very interested in it and I'm sure he'll do it. If not, Effie will pull the trigger. She has already proved herself brave enough to do it during practice, and I admire her for it. My previous assistants were far too squeamish, but it is always better if it is not my assistant who fires the shot but someone else, otherwise the audience may think they have been conned."

So it had been settled that Edward would

point and fire the gun, although of course only he, Thomas, Rose, Effie and Gandini would know that he had been pre-selected to do the deed. Rose had tried to get Effie to explain to her exactly how the trick worked, but she had refused to tell her.

"It would just spoil it for you," said Effie, "knowing what Mr Gandini calls the mechanics of it. Just enjoy the illusion."

"But Gandini isn't actually going to catch the bullet between his teeth, is he?"

Effie snorted with laughter. "Rosie, I know Mr Gandini is a remarkably gifted conjuror, but do you honestly think he has iron teeth? The point is to make people believe that he has. That's the fun of it."

"But aren't you scared?" pressed Rose.

Effie shook her head. "I'm completely confident that nothing will go wrong. Trust me, it will be champagne and lemonade on the house tonight."

Now the hall was humming with excitement as Rose took her seat next to Thomas. Lydia slipped into the seat next to Edward and gave him a beaming smile, and then turned to Rose and smiled too, a melting, unaffected greeting.

Edward had turned and was talking to someone behind him.

"Lydia," said Rose quietly, deciding to seize her chance. "I've been meaning to apologise to you since the day the inspector was here announcing Amy's suicide."

"Whatever for?" asked Lydia lightly.

Rose bit her lip. "It's just that I feel bad. I accidentally overheard you and Stratford-Mark talking in the prop store that day. I'm sorry, it was obviously a private conversation about a private arrangement, and not meant for other ears."

For a second there was a tiny frozen silence, and then Lydia said smoothly, "There is nothing for you to apologise for, Rose. Our conversation was of no consequence. I was merely expressing my desire to Stratford-Mark to give my Lady Macbeth opposite Edward, and not him. He is far too old and unfit. Unsurprisingly, Stratford-Mark was not at all happy and insisted on holding me to our agreement." She gave a laugh that sounded like a mountain waterfall. "It does not matter. Edward and I will have many, many opportunities to act opposite each other in the future. And it does not matter, Rose, that you accidentally heard us." She said the word accidentally as if she had smothered it in butter in order to help it slip down more easily, which made Rose turn bright pink. She was relieved when Thomas leaned across to talk to Lydia.

Rose imagined that once they were married, Edward and Lydia would indeed constantly perform together. She looked around. Campion's had never looked so beautiful and vibrant. The increased revenues of recent weeks had meant that Thomas had been able to repair the gilt on the mirrors and touch up the eggshell-blue interiors. The place glittered and sparkled. Rose believed it was every bit as beautiful as the Pall Mall, and she knew that when word got round that Gandini was performing the famed bullet catch, the place would heave for weeks to come. Thomas would be able to repay Edward's loan far more quickly than he ever imagined. It was such a turnaround in Campion's fortunes since the beginning of the year.

The only thing that detracted from Rose's pleasure was Aurora's absence. She had not accompanied Edward and Lydia to Campion's. Edward said that she had cried off at the last moment, saying she was not feeling well, but insisting that he and Lydia still go. But when Edward had explained Rory's absence, Rose could see from his frown that he didn't quite believe his daughter's sudden indisposition and was puzzled by her reluctance to come to Campion's, the place she had always professed to love most in the world, and where her two best friends lived. Rose sighed. She had told Effie about what had passed between her and Aurora. Effie had eyed her beadily and said she wasn't at all surprised that Rory was upset.

"You accused her father of being dishonourable," she said. "I did warn you, Rosie." Her voice was sad, not gloating. "Once tonight is over I'll go and see her, and maybe she'll come round. But, Rosie, you've got to promise to drop all this detective business. The man at the Anchor must have been mistaken about seeing Edward with Amy. Just accept that Amy stole the Doomstone and drowned herself because she couldn't live with what she had done. Case closed."

Chastened, Rose nodded.

"Do you think Rory minds very much about Edward marrying Lydia?" asked Effie.

"Yes," said Rose. "She's putting a brave face

on it but I think she's distraught. But what can she do? Edward and Lydia are in love, and it's not any ordinary love. When they met in Edward's dressing room after the first night of *Hamlet* it was like watching two people being struck by lightning at the moment they set eyes on each other. Maybe one day they will fall out of love just as quickly and hate each other with a passion. But for now, Rory must know that if she comes between them in any way, her own relationship with her father might be damaged forever. She has to grit her teeth and bear it, and maybe it will all turn out fine. But I just have the feeling that once she's Lady Easingford, and however much she loves Edward, Lydia may be far less charming than she appears."

Effie shook her head. Rose put her hands up. "All right, Effie, I know. I'm speculating again. I hope I'm wrong and they all live happily ever after together."

Now sitting next to Thomas, Edward and Lydia, and feeling Aurora's absence in the empty chair beside her, Rose wished that she had never heard of the wretched Doomstone. It was as if it had cursed her relationship with Aurora. She sighed. If Effie couldn't repair the fractured friendship, then sooner or later Edward and Thomas were going to find out about the rift between her and Aurora, and when they did it was going to be awkward for the two men. Rose wanted to rush up to Edward and confess how her misplaced suspicions had been the cause, but now was not the moment to do it – the show was about to begin. She glanced around. There were so many familiar faces. Lots of regulars including the Tanner Street boys were out in force in the gallery. Anyone who wasn't needed backstage had slipped into the auditorium to watch. Gandini had asked that the bar stop serving during his act tonight, and most of the bar staff, including Billy Proctor, were crowded around their table. Stratford-Mark had just arrived and heaved himself into the vacant seat at the table, murmuring mournful apologies for his tardiness. Lydia threw him a beatific smile and Stratford-Mark nodded amiably but with his eyes hooded like a watchful hawk.

Rose did a double-take as she spotted Inspector Cliff. What was he doing back at Campion's? There had been much speculation among those working at Campion's that something was afoot, and that the bullet catch was probably going to be performed tonight, but no announcement. Rose wondered how the rumours could have possibly spread all the way to Scotland Yard.

There was Gandini's trademark puff of smoke and spark of flame, and then he emerged from out of the smoke, followed by Effie, who was dressed in a sparkling aquamarine gown. She looked very serious. She carried a red velvet cushion, upon which nestled a pistol. As soon as the audience spotted it, they cried out in excitement. Gandini raised a hand and immediately they fell silent.

"Ladies and gentlemen. My friends. Welcome."

Rose watched Gandini closely. There was something different about him tonight. Rose realised that in the early stages of his performances you could normally spot the crucifying nerves that afflicted him every time he walked on stage. But this evening he seemed remarkably calm and focused, and there were no telltale signs of the sweat and nerves that had characterised the opening moments of his previous performances. He was calm – almost deadly calm, as if a storm was brewing deep behind his sea-green eyes. Rose wondered if something had happened before he came on stage – he was seldom so focused in the very first minutes of his act. Or maybe his demeanour was simply a reflection of the sheer gravity of what he was about to attempt, with all its attendant danger.

Gandini was explaining very clearly what he intended to do. The audience was quieter than the grave, hanging on every word.

"So," concluded Gandini, "someone in this audience will be selected at random. They will be given a bullet. They will mark that bullet in a distinctive way and then they will insert that marked bullet into the barrel of the gun. They will then fire the gun from the auditorium directly at me, and I will catch the bullet in my mouth." He smiled at the audience. "And not a hair on my head will be harmed."

The audience broke out in excited cheers and shouts. Even the Tanner Street boys looked impressed at Gandini's calm bravery. Gandini raised a hand and silence once again cloaked the room.

"Effie, please show the audience the gun."

Effie lifted the gun and held it high in the air so that it caught the light.

"It is an ordinary gun. It has not been tampered with. Would anyone like to examine it, to verify the truth of this statement?"

Some men near the front raised their hands. Effie went over to them and handed them the gun. They examined it and announced their satisfaction that it was not a fake or adapted in any way.

"I want to see it," shouted the Tanner Street boy with the scar on his face, who had pushed his way down from the gallery.

Gandini smiled. "Ah, my young friend, you may examine it by all means." He nodded to Effie, and she gave the unloaded gun to the young man, who looked at it carefully.

"It's no fake," he shouted.

Rose glanced at Thomas. It was clever of Gandini to get the Tanner Street boys on his side.

"But if anyone still thinks that it is, I will give you a little demonstration." Gandini produced two bullets from his pocket, held them up and beckoned Effie over. Then he inserted the bullets into the gun. He nodded again at Effie, who disappeared offstage and returned holding a small Chinese-style pot in each hand.

Effie stood with both arms outstretched,

balancing a pot in either palm. Gandini raised the gun and took aim. Rose sensed Thomas half rising from his seat, a look of panic on his face and the word "no" forming on his lips, but he was too late. Two quick shots rang out and the pots both shattered. Effie hadn't even flinched. There was a shocked silence and then the crowd roared. Thomas settled back in his seat, wiping the sweat from his brow. He was angry.

"He didn't tell me he was planning to take potshots at Effie." Rose placed a hand on his arm to calm him.

"Now," said Gandini, "to the main event." He held the gun up in one hand and produced another bullet. He looked slowly around the audience, fixing them with his gaze. "Who is the man or woman who is brave enough to aim the same loaded gun at me and pull the trigger?" He kneeled and picked up a large shard of pot as if to underline the gravity of what he was saying.

"You, sir?" he asked a man in the front. The man shook his head quickly.

"What about you, madam?" Another head was shaken.

"Mr Campion? Will you oblige me?"

"I must decline, Mr Gandini," said Thomas.

"It wouldn't feel right to go round shooting the artistes." Everyone laughed.

"Mr Stratford-Mark?" The theatre owner looked surprised at being addressed. But then he reached towards the cushion in a surprisingly graceful gesture, picked up the gun and turned it over and over in his hands as if caressing it. He looked up and met Gandini's eye.

"Not me," he said quietly.

"Are there no volunteers? If not I will have to ask my charming assistant, Miss Effie, to do the deed. But I would prefer a volunteer from the audience."

"I'll do it," said Edward quietly, but he didn't sound at all happy at the prospect. Lydia looked surprised. Clearly Edward hadn't shared the plan with her, but she clapped and pressed his hand to her cheek.

"M'lud, I am most honoured," said Gandini with a bow. He walked over to Edward, who rose to his feet. He handed him the bullet and Edward marked it with a spot of red paint and then inserted it in the gun.

As Gandini leaned over to take the gun back again, Rose saw him look directly at Lydia, and she thought she heard him murmur something to her very quietly. She thought he might have whispered the words "I know; I'll stop it", but if he did, nobody else seemed to hear, and it made no impression on Lydia's demeanour. She stared straight ahead, her face a beautiful mask. Gandini placed the gun on the cushion and Effie held it aloft for all to see.

Then he invited Edward to step forward and stand on a marked square on the floor in front of the stage. He made a great play of getting Edward to stand in exactly the right spot. Edward was very pale, as if he now regretted his rashness in volunteering to shoot Gandini. Gandini turned to Effie, who was by his side.

"I will now take my place, and then you will hand the gun to his Lordship and count to three. On the count of three he will fire it directly at my mouth, and I will catch the bullet between my teeth." Gandini turned and walked back on to the stage. All eyes were fixed on him. He turned around to face the audience and stared out back at them, his face and eyes grave. The air was thick with silence. Then he nodded to Effie, who handed the gun to Edward. Edward's hand trembled. He slowly raised the gun as if to take aim. Rose sensed Lydia starting to rise to her feet, Edward's name forming on her lips, but she hesitated as Edward's arm went slack and he dropped the gun. There was a buzz of both disappointment and excitement as the tension broke.

"I'm sorry. I can't do it," said Edward ruefully. The words were barely out of his mouth before Lydia was by his side, swooping down to pick up the fallen pistol. Her head almost collided with Effie's as the woman and girl both reached for the pistol, but Lydia's hand reached for it first and swept it up. All eyes were on Edward.

"I'm sorry, Gandini – I thought I could shoot at you but I can't bring myself to do it. There is too much at stake. What if I killed you? I'd never forgive myself."

Gandini nodded. "I quite understand. It has happened to many men before you. It goes against all human instincts to deliberately shoot at a man in cold blood," he said, but his voice was tight.

He walked to Effie, who was holding the pistol she had rescued from Lydia. He plucked it from her hand and rested it almost reverently on the cushion on the table. The gun gleamed menacingly. If all had gone according to plan, and Edward had fired, Gandini would now be bowing in triumph. But instead he was once more facing the uncertainty of having the gun fired directly at him. Effie ushered Edward and Lydia back to their seats. Edward looked a little bashful; Lydia was unusually ruffled, as if she was flustered. Once they were settled, Gandini gazed around the audience.

"Would somebody else like to volunteer?"

The room fell silent.

"I'll do it," came a voice. Everyone turned to look. It was Billy Procter. He walked to the cushion and picked the pistol up. He weighed it in his hand and turned it over, as if examining it.

"Ah, Mr Proctor," said Gandini with a silky smile. "You are quite sure that you are up to the task?" There was a moment of hesitation in Billy Proctor's demeanour. "Quite, quite certain?" asked Gandini again. Rose saw that the inspector was looking at Billy and frowning.

"Maybe not," said Billy, and he flushed beetroot red and replaced the gun on the cushion, knocking the table so that the pistol clattered to the floor and skidded towards the side of the stage. There were a few whistles of derision but Gandini silenced them with his hand. Tobias Fraggles appeared from the side of the stage, retrieved the gun and placed it back on the cushion. Gandini smiled at Effie.

"Then it appears that my delightful assistant, Miss Effie, will have to step into the breach. I know that she will not falter. Are you willing, my dear?"

"Yes, Mr Gandini. I will do it," said Effie, her voice loud and clear.

The audience cheered. Gandini raised a hand.

"Complete silence, please."

Once again Gandini took his place near the back of the stage. Effie picked up the gun from the cushion and stood in the marked square. She raised the gun and took aim. Thomas shifted uncomfortably in his seat. Lydia's eyes glittered feverishly. Edward was almost wincing. Billy had his eyes half closed.

"One," said Effie confidently.

"Two." Her hand didn't shake.

"Three," she shouted, and as she did so she pulled the trigger and a shot rang out. Gandini staggered back, a look of astonishment on his face.

"Treachery! My assistant! ... My…" he gasped in low voice that only those close to the stage could hear, and he fell forward and lay quite motionless. There was a moment of silence before the first person began to scream.

20

Effie stood like a statue, holding the still-smoking pistol, a look of horror frozen on her face as others, including Rose, raced to the aid of the fallen magician. Then she took a dazed step forward, dropped the gun and ran towards Gandini's body. Rose tried to stop Effie forcing her way through the small crowd of people including Inspector Cliff, Thomas, Edward and Billy Proctor, who were gathered around him creating a human barrier. But Effie was like a wild, distressed animal. She was shouting, "No! No! No!" Gandini had fallen face forward but the inspector, with help from some of the men, was turning the conjuror's prone body over. As they turned Gandini there was a tiny sound and something small, white and bloodied hit the stage floor and began to roll. The inspector stopped it and picked it up. Gandini was lying on his back now, quite clearly dead. There was a small, dark round hole near his left temple, where Rose could just see a few strands of sandyish hair that had grown out. The inspector gazed at the hole and then looked down at the small object in his open palm.

"This is quite clearly what did the damage," he said. "Does anyone recognise it?"

Rose's heart stuttered. She saw Edward turn ashen and Thomas's hand go to his mouth, and then Effie said in a tiny voice, "It's my pearl. My lucky pearl. The one Edward gave me." Effie's hand clutched her neck. The pearl and ribbon were gone. She began to cry, the heart-breaking whimpers of a wounded animal.

"Effie," said the inspector gently, "did you put the pearl in the gun?" Effie shook her head. "Effie, do you have any idea how the pearl got in the gun and who put it there?"

Effie was overcome by weeping. "No."

"Are you quite sure that you couldn't have accidently inserted the pearl into the barrel of the gun?"

Effie's tears turned to anger. "Of course not,"

she said indignantly. "I'd never do such a thing. I know the dangers. Mr Gandini taught me well. I know that putting the pearl in the gun and firing it at someone would be a murderous thing to do."

The word "murderous" hung in the air.

"Effie," said the inspector, "tell me exactly how the trick is supposed to work."

"The marked bullet is placed in the chamber by the volunteer, but then while Gandini is distracting the audience by placing the volunteer in exactly the right place on stage, I substitute the marked bullet for a wax one and slip Gandini the marked bullet."

"So," said the inspector, "when the gun is fired, the wax bullet is ejected but the heat melts it so it causes no damage, even if it hits Mr Gandini?" Effie nodded tearfully. "And you made the substitution after Lord Easingford had loaded the gun with his marked bullet?" Effie nodded again. "And nobody else could have tampered with it?"

Effie shook her head. "Only meself, Gandini, Edward and Lydia touched the gun after it was loaded, and Lydia barely at all. Oh, and Billy Proctor, but I was watching him like a hawk cos

I never much cared for the fellow. And Tobias Fraggles, one of the stagehands. But I had me eye on him too. It would be impossible for all but the most skilled magician to make such a substitution. Not without everyone seeing what was happening."

"And you have no doubts that you loaded a wax bullet, not the pearl?"

But Effie was no longer listening. She had sunk to her knees by Gandini's body and began whispering, "Forgive me, forgive me," over and over.

"Effie," said the inspector, much less gently. "What does Mr Gandini have to forgive you for?"

Effie raised her head, her eyes like pools. "I should have checked again. After the trick was halted when Edward lost his nerve. I should have checked the wax bullet was still in place. Instead I just pulled the trigger. I'm a murderer."

There were protests from all the Campion's folk.

"You're not a murderer, Effie," said Rose. "It was a terrible accident."

"No," said Effie. "Mr Gandini always said that there was no such thing as a fatal accident, only fatal stupidity. It was my fault. I wasn't careful enough and I killed him."

The inspector looked sorrowfully at Effie.

"Effie, what was your relationship like with Mr Gandini? Did you get on well?"

"Yes," whispered Effie. "He was very kind to me."

"Are you telling the truth? Because if that is true, why were Mr Gandini's dying words 'treachery' and 'my assistant'?"

Effie shook her head, bewildered. Another policeman appeared by Inspector Cliff's side. He whispered something in his ear and showed him something in his hand. The inspector looked hard at Effie.

"Effie Madley, I'm arresting you for the murder of Mr Gandini."

There was a howl of protest from Rose, Thomas, Edward and all the Campion's staff. Thomas stepped forward and put his hand on Effie's shoulder, and Rose was suddenly aware that Lydia was now by her side. Lydia flung her arms around Effie in a theatrical gesture of comfort, and even in this moment of turmoil Rose thought how like Lydia it was to claim the centre of attention. Effie said nothing and didn't move, her arms poker straight at her sides, as if she was locked in a world of her own.

"Inspector," said Thomas, "surely you can see that Effie cannot be held responsible…"

The inspector raised a hand to silence him. "Mr Campion. I'm afraid the evidence suggests otherwise. There has been a death, Mr Campion, and I must do my duty. I'm afraid that means I'm also arresting you, Mr Campion, for negligence, and issuing an order for the immediate and indefinite closure of Campion's Palace of Varieties and Wonders."

* ✳ *

Rose sat quite alone in an empty Campion's. The place was deserted, sullen and silent, as if it resented having been abandoned. She had gone to Newgate Prison that morning with Mr Cherryble to try and see Thomas, but without success, and she had also written to Julia Devonish at Holloway asking if she might be permitted to visit Effie, but without much hope of achieving anything. Mr Cherryble had patted her hand and hurried away after their failed Newgate visit, telling her he was sure that he would soon be able to get Thomas released, as the police had no evidence that he had been involved in the shooting of Gandini. He seemed far less confident about securing Effie's release.

"Inspector Cliff says there is some significant evidence against her, although he has not yet divulged what it is, and of course there is the fact that nobody but Effie had the opportunity or skills to tamper with the gun in full sight of the entire Campion's audience." Mr Cherryble shook his head. "It doesn't look good for little Effie, particularly as it is common knowledge that her mother was in Holloway for stealing. It counts against her."

Rose slumped miserably, her head in her hands. She felt useless and helpless and very alone. The thought of poor Effie incarcerated in the very same prison where her mother had been imprisoned and died was unbearable. Surely Inspector Cliff and the police would come to their senses and realise that Effie couldn't possibly be responsible for killing Gandini? But how to explain the fact that Gandini had been shot dead by the pearl that belonged to Effie? The substitution of the pearl for the wax bullet couldn't have been a mistake. Whoever had done it must have known that when the gun was fired, it was certain to kill Gandini. But how had it happened? The only people to touch the gun other than Effie were Edward and Lydia, and Billy Proctor and Tobias, and in his dying words Gandini had appeared to point the finger directly at Effie. But why on earth would she try to kill him?

Could Edward have been responsible? Rose had promised Effie that she would put all thoughts of Edward being involved in the disappearance of the Doomstone out of her mind, and accept that Amy had stolen it and taken it to the bottom of the Thames with her. But she couldn't help thinking that what had happened to Gandini must be connected with the theft of the Doomstone. It was too much of a coincidence to think otherwise. It felt as if the curse of the Doomstone was spreading – so many people present on the night of its disappearance had been affected. Somebody had been prepared to try to kill Lydia to get it, Amy and Gandini were both dead, Jem was lying in hospital seriously beaten up, Effie and Thomas were in prison, Rose's friendship with Aurora was broken, and Campion's itself was closed down indefinitely.

She felt bereft. She had lost Thomas, her

friends, her Campion's "family" and the only place she had ever had to call home. But even so, she knew all this loss was nothing beside what Effie was facing if she was found guilty of killing Gandini. She was pulled from her daze by the sound of knocking at the bolted stage door and her name being called. She ran to the door and slid back the heavy bolt.

Aurora stood there, dressed in everyday street clothes, her hair untidy and a large smudge of soot on her nose. For a second the two girls stared at each other hesitantly, and then they fell into each other's arms, crying.

"Oh, Rosie," wept Aurora. "I had to come. Effie! Thomas! It's like a waking nightmare."

"Yes," whispered Rose. "If I didn't know better I'd think it was something to do with the curse of the Doomstone."

Edward appeared in the yard behind Aurora. His face was serious.

"I had to come too. I have a confession you both need to hear," he said.

21

The three of them had been settled in Thomas's office for several minutes, talking about the terrible events of the previous evening. Edward looked exhausted. He said that he had been questioned by Inspector Cliff long into the night, and that Lydia had been questioned too, and he had glimpsed both Tobias and Billy at the police station as well.

"I got the impression that the inspector was very, very keen that somebody other than Effie could be held responsible for killing Gandini," said Edward wearily. "But from what I gather the police are confident that Effie is the culprit. I don't know if it's true, but I heard that there's a witness and some damning evidence."

"It's madness," said Rose angrily. "Effie

wouldn't hurt a fly."

Aurora had been eyeing her father anxiously. "Edward, you said that you had something to tell us both. What is it?"

Edward looked discomfited. "When Aurora made an excuse not to come to Campion's last night I guessed that you two girls had fallen out," said Edward, "but I didn't know what it was about and I didn't think it was my business. I didn't realise that I was the reason for the row."

Rose blushed deeply and couldn't meet Edward's eye.

"It's all right, Rose. Rory has told me that you thought that I might have had something to do with the disappearance of the Doomstone because somehow you discovered that I had a meeting with Mr Drover, the diamond merchant. Rory said that she had told you my dealings with Mr Drover were only in connection with my forthcoming marriage to Lydia, who, I'm delighted to say, has agreed to become my wife.

"Well, that is true. It was why I denied knowing Mr Drover on the night of Effie's debut with Gandini here at Campion's. I had already been in touch with him about resetting the ring."

Rose glanced at Aurora's pained face. Even

back then her father had already decided to marry Lydia. Rose swallowed hard. To now mention her suspicions about Edward in relation to Amy's disappearance would destroy any lasting reconciliation with Aurora. But Edward saved her from having to say anything.

"All I've told you is true. But I told you that I came here to make a confession, and I hope that neither of you will judge me too harshly. I assure you both that I've had nothing to do with the disappearance of the Doomstone or any subsequent events, including the deaths of Gandini and Amy and the attack on Jem. I too can't help thinking that there is a connection between the Doomstone and everything that's happened since. But…" He took a deep breath. "I was at Rotherhithe and saw Amy on the night she died."

Aurora gasped, but Rose said nothing and, seeing her face, Edward said gravely, "You already knew?"

Rose nodded miserably. "You were identified by a witness. He was quite certain it was you he had seen arguing with Amy on the Devil's Steps."

Aurora frowned. "Rosie, if you already knew

Edward had been with Amy on the night she died, is that why, when you stumbled across Mr Drover visiting my father, you were so convinced he was involved in the theft of the Doomstone?"

Rose nodded even more unhappily.

"And if it had been you, Rory, you would probably have thought the same. It was a perfectly reasonable assumption for Rose to make," said Edward, his eyes solemn and fixed on Rose. "I imagine it made Rose think I might even have been responsible for Amy's death in some way. Perhaps that I am even a murderer."

Rose wanted to protest that she had never thought anything of the sort, but it would be a lie. It was exactly what she had been thinking.

"I never believed that Amy had killed herself," said Rose. "Who takes off their dress and folds it before throwing themselves in the Thames? I thought it far more likely that Amy was murdered. Maybe because she had stolen the Doomstone. We know she had it. The woman at the lodging house had seen it. The question is, did Amy steal it as she said in her note, or was she just keeping it safe for someone else? And if it was the latter, what if they came to get it off her? I thought maybe there had been a quarrel and Amy had drowned, and then it was made to look like suicide. Except … except there was the note that Amy left…" She trailed off, thinking hard.

"The note could be a forgery," mused Edward, "or maybe she was made to write it."

Rose thought back to the room. The way that it felt like a theatre set, the whole thing carefully stage-managed.

"Edward," said Aurora quite sharply. "You still haven't explained why you went to Rotherhithe that night, and what happened between you and Amy."

Rose saw the anxiety on her friend's face. Perhaps all her trust in her father was about to be shattered.

"I know it looks mightily suspicious, Rory. I don't blame you for doubting me. But I was on a rescue mission. When Gandini first arrived at Campion's and heard Jem dabbled in magic, the wizard showed Jem some sophisticated card tricks that he planned to work into an act. But when he watched Jem playing cards with the stagehands he realised that Jem was employing the same tricks he had taught him to cheat at the card games. He'd warned him it was a dangerous ploy, and when Jem persisted, he asked me to have a word with him, which I did on the night of Effie's debut. I tore him off a strip. We thought he would see sense and stop, but later that very same night he went to the Anchor."

"Why did Gandini ask you to talk to Jem?" asked Aurora, something accusatory in her voice. Rose suddenly remembered the first night of *Hamlet* at the Pall Mall, when they had overheard malicious mention that Edward had been losing heavily at the card tables in London society. Edward scanned his daughter's face and his eyes were troubled.

"I could lie to you, Rory, but I promise you that I never have and never will. Gandini had heard some rumours about me. I'm afraid they are not very nice. When we returned to London and I was plunged into London society I felt lost and lonely. I had left all my friends in America. I had you and Thomas and everyone at Campion's, but I still felt very alone. I was introduced, by people who I thought were my friends, but weren't, to a world that seemed exciting. I started playing at the card tables. Those supposed new friends – society people – encouraged me. I suspect that some of their own debts were being written off because they had introduced me, the latest mug. I was dazzled by them wanting to be friends with me and I was stupid. I lost a lot of money very fast.

"Fortunately I came to my senses before it was too late. It was around that time that Stratford-Mark offered me the opportunity to play Hamlet in the hope that the box-office returns would help save the Pall Mall, and I realised in the nick of time that I am not made for a dissolute life. I recognised that I am an actor who just happens to have a title, not a lord who happens to act. My heart lies in theatre, not at the gaming table or at polite soirees."

"Good," said Aurora. "I'll remind you of that if you ever forget again." And father and daughter smiled at each other.

"Although I am prepared to put up with the latter for your and Lydia's sake. I'm told that soirees and tea parties are what ladies like."

"What if I don't want to be a lady?" whispered Aurora.

"Oh, Rory," said Edward. "I don't mind. I just want you to have every opportunity. When Lydia came into our lives, I thought she could help ease your way into society. She seems to know everyone. She may be an actress, but she has an entree into every drawing room in London. I thought maybe you might want that too. Or at least have the chance to see if that's what you wanted. If I was wrong and it's making you unhappy, I'm truly sorry."

Aurora took her father's hand and squeezed it ruefully.

"So what was this rescue mission and how does Amy fit into it?" asked Rose.

"On the night of Effie's debut, when Amy died, Gandini received a note from Jem, begging for help. The lad had got himself into terrible trouble at the Anchor, where he had rushed off to straight after the show, in spite of all he had promised me when I had spoken to him. He'd made a slip and been uncovered as a cheat. Things were turning very nasty. Gandini felt responsible. We discussed it and I offered to go down and rescue the boy, and promise those who felt cheated some financial redress. I told Lydia I had business with Thomas, and as soon as I had put her in a cab I went to Rotherhithe."

"What happened?"

"I went because my own foolishness was still fresh in my mind. But by the time I arrived there

241

was no sign of Jem, and of course at the Anchor they denied he'd ever been there. I hoped that he'd got away and would turn up at Campion's. I decided to walk back along the river in case I found him on the way. That's when I stumbled upon Amy. She was standing on the Devil's Steps. I recognised her instantly from the mustard dress. Her welcome was not warm: it was clear she wasn't at all pleased to see me. I wanted to walk her home, make sure she was safe. I was quite insistent – down by the river at that time of night is no place for a young girl on her own. But she just kept telling me to go away and that she preferred to be outside, because it was so hot and it was cooler by the river. I asked her if she had seen Jem, and she said that she had glimpsed him walking along the river path in the direction of Campion's. Of course, later I realised it was a ruse and she was just trying to make me go away so she could throw herself in the Thames." Edward buried his head in his hands. "I feel so guilty. If I had stayed, maybe I could have saved her. Instead I went after Jem, thinking he was the one who needed my help, and of course I saved neither. Jem, I imagine, had already been beaten up and his broken body dumped in an alley behind Lant Street, and it was probably not long after I left her that Amy threw herself in the river."

"But you didn't actually see her doing it?"

Edward shook his head. "No, of course not. If I'd seen her I'd have dived in after her."

"Did you tell the inspector what you'd seen?"

Edward nodded. "Yes, of course, after Lydia announced that Amy was missing. Gandini was horrified when I told him I had seen Amy on the Devil's Steps. He made me go over exactly what I'd seen several times. He was keen that I should just forget the encounter – he kept talking about the scandal that would ensue if I told the police – but I insisted, even though at that point we didn't know Amy was dead. She was just missing. I went to see the inspector and told him the story of going to rescue Jem and seeing Amy on the steps. I just didn't mention Gandini's involvement."

"So," said Rose slowly, "you were the other witness that the inspector mentioned who had seen Amy on the steps."

Edward nodded, embarrassed. "The inspector thought discretion was a good idea. He said the penny dreadfuls would have a field day with

'Peer of the Realm Sees Suicide Girl' stories."

"But you didn't actually see anything, did you?"

"No, I didn't," said Edward. "After I walked for a few minutes towards Campion's I did turn back, thinking that perhaps I had been unwise to leave Amy, even though she clearly wanted me to clear off. I felt uneasy. But by the time I got close to the Devil's Steps I could see that she wasn't there. That mustard dress sticks out a mile. There was just a boy in the distance walking away down the path in the other direction, and a couple of drunks lurching towards me. I thought she must have gone home. It never crossed my mind that she was in the river. There had been nothing in her demeanour to suggest such a thing. She had seemed irritated, not distressed. So I turned back towards Campion's. If only I'd gone closer! I'd have found her dress on the steps. Perhaps if she had only just gone in the water I might have been able to save her."

There was a loud rap on the door. A messenger stood there with an envelope in his hand addressed to Rose. It was from Julia Devonish, asking her to come to Holloway at once. Rose had been granted a visit to see Effie.

22

Rose and Aurora sat opposite each other in a cab rattling towards Holloway Prison through wisps of yellowish fog. Aurora had insisted on coming, even though she knew that she would have to wait outside the prison. Rose had sent a reply back to Julia to say she was coming at once, and Edward had helped find them a cab. It was another sultry day, close and oppressive, as if someone had sucked all the air out of the city. Even the dogs were listless, and smuts clung to the cab windows making the whole city look bruised.

"You do believe Edward, don't you?" asked Aurora anxiously as they bumped through the parched streets, bouncing over potholes like gouged-out eye sockets.

Rose nodded. Relief flooded Aurora's face.

"I do too. He may be an idiot, but I don't think he had anything to do with the Doomstone's disappearance or Amy's and Gandini's deaths."

"But somebody did," said Rose, frowning, "and probably somebody we know." There was silence for a moment, and then she said, "Rory, I don't want to pry, but what do you mean about Edward being an idiot? Do you mean over the gambling, or is there something else?"

Rory pinked. "Nothing gets past you, Rose Campion."

"Except it does – I reckon that the answer to the disappearance of the Doomstone and these terrible deaths is staring me in the face, but I just can't see it. I'm being blind."

"Like my dad is blind in love, so he only sees the good in Lydia, and not the vanity, the selfishness, the way she manipulates him to get her way and all the little unkindnesses," said Rory very quietly.

"Is she so awful? I thought you admired her. Do you hate her, Rory?"

"I don't hate her, and she's not awful, just self-obsessed, and obsessed with Edward, just as he is with her. If you're suggesting that Lydia will be a wicked stepmama from out of a fairy story, then you're wrong. As long as I'm biddable and don't cross her I'm sure she'll be quite delightful. She may even enjoy showing me off like a pretty little lapdog. But when Edward and Lydia are married I think I'll be spending much more time with you at Campion's, unless of course she packs me off to that awful school, Miss Pecksniff's Academy for Young Ladies, that you ran away from after Thomas sent you there."

Rose grinned. "Yes, poor Thomas thought he could turn me into a lady, but pigs will fly first." She sighed. "I do hope Mr Cherryble gets him released from Newgate. Campion's feels desolate without him." She looked at her friend, relieved that she could call Aurora that again. "Maybe this terrible business with Thomas's and Effie's arrests will slow things down with Edward and Lydia and they won't be in such a rush to marry."

"I hope so too," said Aurora. "I know I'm being selfish, and of course I want Edward to be happy, but I can't help feeling that it's unfair that he and I had only just found each other and were getting to know each other, and then Lydia came between us."

"Edward clearly adores her. Do you think she loves him?" asked Rose. "My impression is that she does, she's not pretending."

"Oh yes. That's the saving grace. I'm sure that Lydia is thrilled that Edward has a title and a fortune, but I don't think that's why she's marrying him. It was what the French call a *coup de foudre*. A thunderbolt. Even Amy said it was true love, and she was always very cynical about anything to do with Lydia. Quite indiscreet at times when Lydia was in a mood and she was in a mood with Lydia. It's strange, because although Lydia was the employer and Amy her dresser, and Lydia used her more like a ladies' maid, I sometimes got the impression that it was Amy who was watchful of Lydia – as if she had something over her."

Rose suddenly gave a little bounce of excitement. "Maybe she did! Maybe she knew something about Lydia's past? Maybe she found something out?"

Aurora smiled ruefully. "Well, everyone knows that Lydia wasn't born a lady. One of the reasons I admired her at first was because she made everyone she met forget it. She may not be the world's greatest actress, but she played the part of a lady to perfection. I thought if she could do it, maybe if I was more like her people would forget where I came from too, and that eventually they would accept me and stop whispering about me everywhere I went."

Rose took her friend's hand. Aurora's eyes were swimming, and she brushed the tears away angrily.

"Maybe you're right and Amy did have something on Lydia. But why would she bother? She had the Doomstone. She had stolen it from around Lydia's neck, almost slitting Lydia's throat in the process, and it was worth a fortune. Why hang around being bossed about by Lydia when she could have sold it and gone anywhere she liked?"

"Except selling something like the Doomstone would be hard. Remember what Effie told us. No fence would touch it. You would have to wait months to dispose of something like that, unless you had really serious connections in the criminal world, or a buyer already lined up. Maybe she was just biding her time." Rose shook her head. "I'm convinced that Gandini's death must be connected to its disappearance too."

"Maybe Amy and Gandini were in league with each other," said Aurora.

Rose bounced in her seat, and it wasn't because of a pothole. "Of course," she said excitedly. "That must be it! On the night of Effie's debut, Amy demonstrated that she could do magic. Maybe she and Gandini had an arrangement? While he distracted everyone in the room, she stole the Doomstone from around Lydia's neck. Maybe somebody found out and killed Amy and tried to make it look like suicide, and then killed Gandini?"

"Or," said Aurora, "maybe Amy stole the Doomstone, and then Gandini killed Amy to get it, and then somebody else killed him to get it."

Rose nodded. "The one thing I'm certain of is that poor Effie has simply been caught up like a fly in a spider's web."

They arrived at the prison and went straight to the gatehouse, where Julia Devonish was waiting. She immediately murmured her commiserations about Thomas's arrest.

"A dreadful business. But I'm sure Mr Cherryble will secure his release. It's little Effie

I'm most concerned over." Julia recognised Aurora immediately as Edward's daughter. "I will authorise a visit from both of you," she said. "I'm afraid that things are looking very grim for Effie. The poor child is distraught. I'm worried about her state of mind. She keeps saying that she's cursed."

The three girls were huddled around a small table in Julia Devonish's office, holding hands so tightly it was as if they had been glued together. Effie's sludge-grey prison smock matched the colour of her face.

"I'm afraid," she whispered. "I'm afraid I'm going to die in this place just like my mother. Maybe it's just another form of justice. My mother took the blame for the crime I committed, and now fate has caught up with me. I'm here where I should have been all along. I'm doomed."

Rose shook her head fervently. "That isn't justice, Effie, not even close. You didn't kill Gandini so you shouldn't be tried for the crime, particularly not when whoever did kill him is walking around free."

"I as good as killed him," said Effie mournfully. "And I got Campion's closed down and Thomas arrested. It's all my fault."

"Effie," said Rose. "Don't worry about Thomas and Campion's, just focus on your own situation. Edward is going to pay for lawyers to argue your case in court. They will want to talk to you so they can prepare their defence. I want you to think very carefully and go over everything that happened the night Gandini died."

Effie frowned. "I've bin over it and over it. With the police. And in me head. The Blues asked me about Edward and Lydia, but I told them neither of them could have made the switch. Nor Tobias or Billy. I would have seen unless one of them is the world's greatest magician and I was struck blind."

"Was there anything unusual about that night?" asked Aurora.

"We was doing the world's most dangerous magic trick. It weren't a normal evening. But apart from Edward flunking pulling the trigger – an' Mr Gandini had warned me it could happen, it often does, and the assistant has to step in to do the deed – everything was going to plan. If anything, Mr Gandini was much calmer than usual. He weren't sweating like he normally does. It were as if all his stage fright melted away like a penny lick."

"I noticed that too," said Rose. "It was as if on that last night he had finally conquered his nerves. He was so calm, almost frighteningly so. Almost as if he was angry about something."

Effie nodded vigorously. "It felt like that to me. I told the police that and it ain't helped. They think he were angry with me. They keep trying to say I killed him in a rage because we had a row before we went on stage." She began to weep. "But we didn't. I went down to his dressing room as I normally did. He was in a right state. Nerves worse than usual. So I just did what I always did: chatted away to distract him."

"What did you talk about?"

Effie shrugged. "Nothing important. I told him about Ophelia getting stuck up the chimney an' how you, Rosie, climbed up to rescue her and came down so covered in soot that one of the ballet girls thought you were a ghost. I told him how Belle Canterbury's mum has taken a turn for the worse and nobody thinks she'll last until the start of the pantomime season. I told him there are rumours that Stratford-Mark is confident that the Pall Mall will be saved and has told his creditors that he will pay them before the end of the week…" She blushed before continuing, "I know it was supposed to be a secret but I was running out of things to say so I told him about Eddie and Lydia getting married, and how I thought it was the most romantic thing in the world to marry someone you had only known for a few weeks. Then we got the call and went on stage, an' the whole thing unfolded like a bad dream."

Rose was frowning. "If only we knew what had made him angry. You're right – it can't have been anything you said, Effie. It's all just innocuous tittle-tattle."

"Unless," said Aurora slowly, "he wasn't angry with someone else, but with himself, for some reason we don't know."

Rose shot Aurora a quizzical glance. "Are you suggesting that maybe Gandini wanted to die for some reason, and he swapped the bullet himself? Deliberately?"

"You mean he murdered himself?" shrieked Effie incredulously. "That would be a rum do.

An' I don't believe it. Mr Gandini was sometimes sad, but he was looking forward to retiring from the stage. He'd made me promise not to tell anyone, but he said that his Campion's run would be his last. He just couldn't cope with the stage fright no longer. It were killing him, and he was going to leave performing behind and live in a little pink cottage by the sea. He told me if I wanted to carry on being a magician's assistant he would try and find me a job cos I was that good at it. But I told him that it was ever so nice of him but I wouldn't ever leave Campion's. It was me home."

She burst into tears. "Now I'll never see Campion's agin. I'll be locked up here forever. I'd be better off drowned at the bottom of the Thames like poor Amy, or shot in the head like kind Mr Gandini. I can't bear it." Tears poured down her cheeks. "You don't have any idea of how horrible it is here. There's this woman, everyone calls her the Duchess, and once she heard I was from Campion's and in here for shooting Gandini, she don't leave me alone. Keeps asking me about him. She wants to know what he looked like. How he spoke. If he had anyone with him. I tells her naught but that he was a real gentleman, but she won't let it go. She frightens me. If the hangman's noose don't get me I reckon she will."

Effie's sobs reached a crescendo just as the door opened and Julia Devonish walked in. Effie was silenced mid-sob by Julia's serious face.

"I have news and I'm afraid it's not good. Your trial is to start tomorrow, Effie."

"But it can't," said Rose. "Effie's lawyers won't have had time to prepare their defence."

"There is nothing that can be done to stop it. The police believe that it is an open-and-shut case and so can be dealt with quickly," said Julia, and Rose could read the sadness in her eyes.

"See," said Effie bitterly. "I'm cursed. And it's all to do with the Doomstone."

Julia went with Rose and Aurora to the gatehouse. Through the window, Rose glimpsed a man striding away who she was certain was Billy Proctor. She grabbed Aurora's arm and whispered, "That's Billy Proctor. What's he doing here?"

Julia heard. "Yes, that is Mr Proctor," she said smoothly, but Rose could see she was disconcerted. "He had business here. But it's nothing to do with Effie. He was seeing a woman known as the Duchess."

Rose said nothing but she felt excited. She had been right to be suspicious of Billy Proctor and his connections with the Duchess, particularly as this Duchess also seemed especially interested in Gandini's death.

As soon as Rose got back to Campion's she sent a note to Inspector Cliff telling him about Billy, but she got no reply. She wished Thomas was here. He would know what to do to make the inspector take her suspicions seriously. She went to Newgate Prison in the hope of gaining admission and seeing Thomas, but she was turned away without even the comfort of a smile.

24

Rose and Aurora sat in the courtroom throwing encouraging glances at Effie, who stood in the dock looking as forlorn as an abandoned dog. It was unbearably hot and the dark wooden panelling and formality of the court were oppressive. The elderly judge, forbidding in his wig and robes, kept sighing wearily. The way he kept glancing at Effie made Rose think that he had already decided she was guilty, and was irritable that he had to sit through the evidence being presented against her, and just wanted to pronounce sentence so he could retire for his lunch. The lawyers appointed by Edward had expressed their dismay at the hurried nature of the proceedings, and asked for more time to consult with their client, but their pleas had been dismissed by the judge. Every time Effie's defence lawyer stood to speak the judge looked ever more crotchety. His hand made an unconscious circular motion as if he was trying to hurry him on.

"This isn't fair, this isn't justice," hissed Rose loudly to Aurora after Effie's lawyer had been cut off by the judge mid-stream. The judge glared in their direction. Rose looked around the courtroom. Edward was missing as he was still trying to secure Thomas's release from Newgate, but there was a good turnout from Campion's in the public gallery, led by Lottie and Tessa and some of the other ballet girls, and most of the bar staff. Even Billy Proctor was there. She had caught him exchanging a word with Inspector Cliff on the steps on the way into the court and she felt annoyed that the inspector had so clearly ignored her note. For a horrible moment she had wondered whether Billy might be giving evidence against Effie; she wouldn't put it past him, always lurking around backstage where he wasn't supposed to be and spying on people. But clearly her suspicions had been misplaced, or he wouldn't be in the courtroom now.

The prosecution were calling a witness. Tobias Fraggles entered the court and made his way into the witness box. He kept his eyes on the floor, and an ugly flush spread across his handsome face as expressions of surprise and hisses came from the public gallery. He took the oath and stood uncomfortably in the box as the prosecution lawyer quizzed him about his name and address, and established that he had been at Campion's working backstage on the night of Gandini's death.

"Mr Fraggles, on the night in question did you go to Mr Gandini's dressing room just before the show?"

Tobias cleared his throat. "Yes, sir," he said, still not raising his head.

"Why was that?" demanded the lawyer.

"I 'ad a question for the wizard 'bout the placing of the table. I wanted to make sure I 'ad it right. The wizard was a right stickler for fings being just so. 'E don't like anyfing out of place." Tobias was looking and sounding more confident.

"And did you ask Mr Gandini about the table?"

"No," said Tobias shaking his head.

"And why was that, Mr Fraggles?"

"Cos when I got to Mr Gandini's dressing room there was a right racket goin' on. I could 'ear it through the door. I dinna want to interrupt."

"Could you identify the speakers?"

"One of 'em was the wizard. He kept saying, 'calm down, calm down.'"

"And the other?" asked the lawyer.

"It was her, Effie Madley," said Tobias, pointing straight at Effie. "I'd know 'er voice anywhere."

"And what was the accused saying?"

Tobias looked straight ahead and said loudly, in an unwavering voice, "I hate you."

The lawyer put his head on one side like a curious bird. "Anything else?"

Tobias nodded. "One day, Gandini, you're going to get what's coming to you: a bullet through the forehead."

There were gasps.

"No," shouted Rose. "That can't be true."

"Silence!" roared the judge. "Or I will clear the court. I will have anyone who interrupts removed."

Rose's mind was racing. It didn't sound like Effie, and unless Effie had been feigning a respect and affection for Gandini all along, it was at odds with the way that she had always talked about the magician – not least because she always gave him the courtesy of calling him Mr Gandini. She desperately wanted to get the attention of the defence lawyer, but he was already on his feet and cross-examining Tobias, who was sticking to his story like a dog with a juicy bone. Rose had to admit that he sounded both consistent and convincing. The defence lawyer was finishing his examination of the witness.

"Mr Fraggles, do you have any grudge against the accused?"

"None at all," said Tobias smoothly. "She liked to try and 'elp out in the workshop. She'd try and mend fings. But course she's only a girl and she ain't got no strength and the brains for that sort of fing. I always tried to 'elp her best I could, but she's got a right temper on her. She threatened me once with an 'ammer."

There were more gasps from the gallery, quickly hushed. Rose thought she might explode. She knew for certain that the man was lying. If only Thomas was here to be a witness. He would set the judge straight about Effie's character. She felt Aurora's calming hand on her shoulder, but Rose was anything but calm. Effie was looking at her with the beseeching eyes of a kicked mongrel who was about to be dropped in the river.

The next witness had been called. It was the policeman who had been present on the night of Gandini's death, and who had discreetly shown Inspector Cliff something that he found. The prosecution lawyer asked a number of questions before building to the climax of his cross-examination. He produced a small folded piece of paper, and it was passed to the policeman.

"I want you to examine this piece of paper carefully and tell the court if you are certain that this is the piece of paper you found when you searched Mr Gandini's dressing room in the minutes after his death."

The defence lawyer looked puzzled. It was clearly the first time he had heard about the piece of paper.

"Is this the piece of paper you found in the dressing room?" repeated the prosecution lawyer.

"Yes, sir, it is."

"Will you read it out, please?"

The policeman cleared his throat. "Gandini,

you is the walking dead. Watch yer back. EM."

Rose starred at Aurora, her excitement growing. The note was clearly a fake. Whoever had written it didn't know that Effie couldn't read or write. Her mind lurched to the note she had found in Amy's room. Whoever had killed Amy must also be responsible for Gandini's murder, and was now trying to frame Effie for the crime! The words rose from her throat.

"This is ridiculous. It's clearly a fake because—"

But she got no further. The judge pinned her with his furious gaze and summoned the court ushers, who yanked Rose from the courtroom, her protests drowned by the uproar all around her. Rose was bundled protesting through corridors and the grand hall and pushed out on to the court steps. She was weeping in frustration at the court system and her own stupidity. If she had only kept her mouth shut and sent a note to the defence lawyers, then perhaps they would have been able to prove Effie's inability to read and write by demonstrating her lack of skill in the witness box. Although perhaps the cranky old judge would simply conclude that she was feigning. Rose began to feel that Effie had been right when she had said that she was doomed.

She didn't know what to do but wait until Aurora came to find her. There was a big crowd gathered outside the courtroom, all clearly awaiting the verdict, some with a salacious excitement. In a daze Rose wandered among them. Two women beside her were talking loudly.

"Will she get the death sentence if she's found guilty?"

"Too young," said the other, sounding disappointed. "But she deserves it, the little minx. It was cold-blooded murder."

"I wonder why she did it?" her friend replied.

"We'll probably never know," said the other shaking her head.

The crowd was growing. Rose felt herself jostled. This kind of crowd was prime territory for pickpockets. She peered around suddenly with the odd feeling that she was being observed from very close by. She thought she caught a glimpse of gooseberry-green eyes in a pale face, but lost sight of them in the crowd.

At that moment, people began to push their way out of the courtroom and a boy came running out through the doors shouting at the top of his voice: "Guilty! The verdict is guilty! Life imprisonment."

The cry went up through the crowd. Rose suddenly felt faint. She saw Lydia and Edward making their way through the crowd towards her. They had obviously arrived just as the verdict had been announced.

"There you are," said a man sagely. "Such an innocent-looking little thing, and a murderess. Maybe she knocked off that other one too, the one who is supposed to have drowned herself and the Doomstone in the river."

Amy! Rose's heart began to hammer in her chest and she started looking frantically around, searching the faces of the crowd, looking again for those distinctive gooseberry-green eyes. In the far distance over the other side of the square she could see a lanky girl. Her back was to Rose and she was pushing her way through the far side of the crowd away from Rose as if panicked by something.

Rose stared. It couldn't be! Could it? Rose was about to cry out, "Amy!" when she heard her own name being shouted. It was Edward. He and Lydia were coming from the other side of the square and were almost upon her. She saw Aurora tear out of the court building and stumble down the steps to join them, blind with tears. Rose glanced back again to where she was sure that she had seen Amy, but there was no sign of her. Could she be mistaken? She must be! Rose's heart was beating a tattoo. Around her the crowd had taken up the cry "guilty", and were chanting it as if they were trying to taunt her with the word. Aurora, Edward and Lydia were all closer now, determinedly pushing their way towards her. Edward was weeping openly. When they reached Rose, Aurora and Edward wrapped their arms around her and the three of them stood for a moment together. When they broke apart, Lydia was gazing at her with pin-sharp eyes.

"My! You are as white as a sheet, Rose. You look as if you've just seen a ghost."

25

Rose held both of Effie's hands in one of the cells under the courtroom. Effie had cried herself out and her tears had subsided into hiccups. She and Rose had been granted a few snatched minutes together before Effie would be taken to Holloway to begin her life sentence. Rose wondered how many years it might be before they saw each other again. However sympathetic Julia Devonish was to Effie's plight, she wouldn't find it so easy to bend the visiting rules for a convicted felon found guilty of murder.

"Effie, we will get you out. Edward is already talking to the lawyers. There must be grounds for appeal. Nobody challenged what Tobias Fraggles had to say, or explained that he had a grudge against you because you mended something he said was broken beyond repair. If only Thomas had been here to set the record straight! If only they had called you to the witness stand so you could have told them."

Effie shook her head. "Nah. I were too nervous. I'd never have got them words out. Eddie's lawyer told me to go in the box. But I knew all them clever lawyers would bamboozle me. I'd have stammered and stuttered. They'd have made me look stupid and a liar. It would have bin a waste of time. Me card was marked. I was going to be found guilty no matter how many fancy lawyers Ed paid for. He should have saved his money."

Rose wanted to shake Effie for being so passive and accepting of her fate. "Effie, you've got to help us fight this miscarriage of justice. You know that's what Thomas would say if he was here. That note is clearly a fake. You have to tell them that you didn't write it, and that you couldn't have written it because you can't write."

Effie gazed at Rose, her eyes pools of sadness. "There's the thing, Rosie. I can write now. And read. I was just biding me time and I was going to surprise you all when the moment was right.

I couldn't wait to see your and Thomas's eyes. Mr Gandini had bin teaching me. He said if I wanted to be a proper magician's assistant then I had to learn to read and write. Insisted it was essential for the job. He used a big word for it. Said I needed the 'requisite' skills. Said he did such a good job with the training that some of his previous assistants had become almost as skilled as he was himself. He was ever so patient. It were one of the reasons I liked him so much. He never had a cross word, however much I struggled with the reading and writing, and I have struggled cos it sometimes feels like them letters have got a grudge against me. But I didn't give up. So you see I could have written that note. The police took a sample of me doing my writing and they said it were near enough, though that note don't look nothing like my writing to me."

"But you didn't write it, did you?" asked Rose.

Effie shook her head. "Nah. I would never have done anything to hurt Mr Gandini." Then she added darkly, "It would have been no way to repay his kindness to me."

"But somebody did, Effie, and that somebody is still free."

Effie shivered. "Maybe I'm safer in prison. With Gandini and poor little Amy dead, who's going to be next?" She peered at Rose, whose face had betrayed her at the mention of Amy's name. "What is it, Rosie?"

Rose gave an anxious little laugh. "You're going to think me daft as a hatter, Effie, but I thought I saw Amy in the crowd outside the courtroom."

"But Amy's at the bottom of the Thames, Rosie. She can't be running around outside the court." Effie laughed nervously. "Maybe you're seeing them ghosts again. Like when you saw poor, murdered Ned Dorset."

Rose shook her head, frowning. "This was different, Effie. I wasn't seeing a ghost."

"You was all shook up, Rosie, after being turfed out of the court like that. Your nerves probably got the better of you."

"No," said Rose indignantly. "You think I was seeing things. But I know I saw her, and I'm certain she was flesh and blood. Those gooseberry-green eyes."

"Yes, just like poor Mr Gandini's eyes."

Rose jumped up so suddenly she knocked over her chair.

"Of course! That's it! Amy! Gandini! They must be father and daughter. How stupid of me! Why didn't I see it before? It was staring me in the face. Those eyes, the long lanky body. Their colouring was so different I didn't see it."

"We know Mr Gandini dyed his hair and beard," said Effie excitedly.

"Yes!" said Rose. "It must have been to disguise the fact that he and Amy were related." She gasped. "And we know that Amy had conjuring skills. We saw her using them, and we also know she had the Doomstone. It can only mean that Amy and Gandini were in league together and while he distracted the crowd she stole the Doomstone from around Lydia's neck, almost murdering the poor woman in the process." Rose's mind was racing. "But maybe Amy didn't want to share with her dad. So she must have faked her own death, and then for some reason – maybe just pure, simple greed – she decided she had to kill her own father." Rose bounced excitedly up and down on the balls of her feet. "When with his dying breath Gandini said 'my assistant', he wasn't pointing the finger at you, but at Amy! She must have assisted him in the past."

Effie didn't look convinced. "Hang on, Rosie," said Effie. "We are talking about Amy here. Little, anxious Amy who kept herself to herself. Aren't you getting a bit ahead of yourself? Even if Amy did fake her own death and escape with the Doomstone, why would she want her own father dead? And how on earth did she arrange it in such a way to frame me when she weren't even there? However good a magician she was, she would have had to have been at Campion's that night. I don't see how she could have possibly managed it without everybody noticing that someone who was supposed to be drowned at the bottom of the river was hanging around and substituting a wax bullet for the pearl that was hanging safely round me neck."

"She must have had an accomplice! I'm going to pay a little visit to Tobias Fraggles. He lied in court in order to get you convicted. I want to know why."

"Oh, Rosie, you watch yourself. We don't want any more dead bodies," said Effie, as two female warders appeared at the door and began to unlock it. It was time for Effie to be taken to Holloway. Rose held her friend tight.

"Don't give up hope, Effie. One way or another we are going to prove your innocence and get you back home to Campion's."

26

"Edward and Lydia are going ahead with the wedding?" repeated Rose slowly, her voice utterly incredulous. Aurora nodded. "Even with poor Effie convicted only a few hours ago and locked up in Holloway Prison? And they are going to celebrate a wedding? It's not right! It's so insensitive." She was shouting.

Rose had arrived back to find Thomas had got to the music hall shortly before her, having just been released from the gaol. His face was haggard and his eyebrows were knitted with worry. Campion's was still forbidden to open and he was clearly distraught over Effie's conviction. He put a hand on Rose's shoulder.

"Calm down, Rosie, you are not helping. If I was Edward it wouldn't be what I'd want, either," he said gently. "But it was always going to be the quietest of weddings. Just Aurora, you, Effie and me and Stratford-Mark to act as the witnesses at the ceremony, and a few friends from the Pall Mall. No big do after. I know it seems inappropriate in the circumstances, but even though little Effie is in Holloway the world still turns. When would it no longer be too soon? Tomorrow? Next week? Next year? As we always say…"

"…the show must go on," said Rose finishing the sentence for him, the sarcasm evident in her voice. Thomas shook his head and walked away, and Rose looked after him, feeling guilty. He was clearly exhausted and had plenty to worry about without her adding to his woe.

"Edward wanted to cancel. To rearrange for some other time," said Aurora quietly, "but Lydia wasn't having it. She got quite hysterical, like a mad thing. She said the arrangements were made and they should go ahead. Edward took the line of least resistance: he always does what he can to please her. I'd think she'd cast a spell on him if it wasn't for the fact that she clearly adores him as much as he loves her." She looked into her friend's furious face. "You will come, won't you, Rosie? I know Edward would be so sad if you were missing as well as Effie. Me too. I need you there."

Rose nodded. "Of course. I'll be at St Olave's for ten p.m. I'll even put on my best dress for it. But first I'm going to visit Tobias Fraggles and see what he has to say for himself."

Aurora's eyes clouded. "Is that a good idea, Rose?"

"Yes," said Rose firmly, and she told Aurora what had happened outside the court, and how she was certain that she had seen Amy and was convinced that Amy was Gandini's daughter and former assistant, had faked her own death and was responsible for killing her own father. "I think that Tobias Fraggles was her accomplice. Why else would he tell those lies against Effie in court?"

Aurora's eyes had grown bigger and bigger. "We should tell Inspector Cliff."

"He's not going to believe me, Rory. He thinks Amy is dead and he's caught Gandini's murderer: Effie. He'll just say I'm making it up to help her. But if I confront Tobias, maybe I'll get to the truth and he'll lead me to Amy. Then I can tell Inspector Cliff. Present the entire thing on a plate to him. He'll have to listen."

Aurora's face was a picture of anxiety. "At least let's tell Thomas."

Rose shook her head. "I don't want to worry him. It's as if those few nights in prison have knocked all the stuffing out of him. I'll tell him after I've visited Tobias."

"So you want us to drop by for a chat with a man who may be a cold-blooded murderer?"

Rose grinned. "Yes, and I imagine that as you used the word 'us' you are planning on coming with me."

"I can't say I'm thrilled at the prospect," said Aurora. "But I can hardly let you confront him on your own. I'll come with you, but only because I think you are so mad that you shouldn't be allowed out on your own. But I need to be back in Silver Square by four thirty because I have the final fitting for my bridesmaid's dress. So we'd better hurry."

* ✶ *

Rose and Aurora made their way down the grimy street. The heat had held the city so long in its sweaty grip that even the dogs didn't bother to raise their heads as the girls passed by. Rose had told Aurora about Gandini teaching Effie to read and write, which meant that her illiteracy couldn't be used in her defence.

"Oh, Rose, I do hope that you are on to something," said Aurora sadly, "otherwise things look really bleak for Effie."

She wiped the sweat away from her brow. There was a distant rumble of thunder. Rose glanced up at the sky, which was like a heavy black saucepan lid, pressed down on the overheated city.

"It will be a relief when it breaks," she said as they stopped outside a faded blue front door.

"You're sure this is the place?"

Rose nodded. She had memorised the address read out in the courtroom. They knocked. There was a moment's silence, and then a heavy tread and a thickset man opened the door. His eyes were blue and watery. He was breathing heavily. Time had had its way with his face, but there was a striking similarity to Tobias.

"Mr Fraggles?"

"Who's asking?"

"I'm Rose Campion and this is Rory; we're both from Campion's music hall."

The man peered towards them and his expression softened. "You're them two girls who do that bicycle act, ain't you? That's a good'un, says my Tobias. One of the best acts on the bill. Better even than that wizard. The one that got shot."

"Oh," said Rose. "That's nice of Tobias. You should come and see it."

The man gave a little laugh as if at a private joke. "I don't get out much."

"In fact, it's Tobias we're looking for. Is he home?"

The man shook his head. "You ain't the only one looking for him this afternoon. I was 'specting him back for his dinner. He was at that court this morning. But it's not like him not to be back for his dinner." He shook his head. "But he's bin that unreliable and dopey recently. I wonder whether he's got a girl, but he ain't telling if he has, however much I quiz him. I'd like to see him settled before I go. Me heart ain't strong. Shall I tell him you called?"

"We'll try again later," said Rose. They turned to leave when Rose spun round. "You said we're not the only ones asking. Has he had other callers?"

"Yes," said the man. "There was a girl knocked earlier."

"What did she look like?" asked Rose urgently. The man gave a rueful smile, and Rose suddenly understood that the man was blind. She felt a fool. She hadn't noticed. "I'm so sorry, I hadn't realised you couldn't see."

"I'll take that as a compliment," said the man. "It's a matter of pride that people don't notice, and when I'm in me own home they often don't. I enjoy surprising them. Sometimes I think the entire world is blind and I see far more than them."

"We're sorry to have bothered you," said Rose.

"I'll tell you this for free," said Mr Fraggles. "The girl who knocked. She sounded pretty."

Rose and Aurora walked slowly away towards the river.

"That's ridiculous," said Aurora. "How can someone sound pretty?"

"I don't know, but maybe he was right and when you are blind you can see things differently. Maybe you can tell someone's pretty from the confidence with how they walk and talk," said Rose. "Tobias is sure to come back sooner or later. We can intercept him when he does."

Aurora nodded, although she was clearly anxious about the time. "Maybe it wasn't Amy who was looking for Tobias."

"Who else could it have been? If we wait here, maybe she'll come back too and we can catch both of them together."

"And then what are we going to—"

Aurora didn't finish the sentence because there was a commotion at the far end of the street by the river. A woman was screeching at the top of her voice and calling for the police. The girls hurried down to the river's edge, where a small crowd was beginning to gather. Rose ran ahead and looked down into the water. Tobias Fraggles was bobbing on his back. His eyes were quite as sightless as his father's. But Tobias was dead. The bloodied gash on his throat was still bright crimson. Rose turned away feeling sick.

"Amy must have got to him before we did."

Aurora tugged at Rose's sleeve. "You are to go straight to Scotland Yard and tell Inspector Cliff everything you know. No arguing. I'll drop you off in a cab on my way to Silver Square."

Rose nodded, made unusually biddable by the shock of seeing Tobias's corpse.

It took an age to find a cab, but they hailed one at last. But then they got caught behind an overturned dray cart and over forty minutes had elapsed before they eventually rolled into the broader avenues of Whitehall. Rose was very quiet and as they neared Scotland Yard tears began to fall down her cheeks. The cumulative shock of the last few days had got to her.

"Here," said Aurora, proffering a handkerchief and putting her arm around her friend.

"It's all right," said Rose. "I've got my own. She plunged her hand into her pocket, and felt something that shouldn't be there. It was a postcard. A seaside scene of little fishermen's cottages drawn in charcoal. Just like the one she had found in Amy's room. She had given that card to the inspector so how had this one got in her pocket?

"What is it?" asked Aurora.

Rose turned the postcard over. On the other side in hastily scribbled script were the words: "Save me! For God's sake, help me." The words were signed with a name: Amy.

"See!" said Rose. "I wasn't going mad or seeing ghosts. I did see Amy, and she must have slipped this in my pocket without me noticing. It's proof that she's still alive!"

"But I don't understand why she would do such a thing," said Aurora. "Why would she risk drawing attention to herself? If she killed Gandini or arranged his murder it would be better for her if everyone continued to think she was dead. It's the perfect crime. Nobody's ever going to suspect a ghost of murder and no policeman has ever successfully arrested one."

"That's true," said Rose, her brow puckered. "But maybe she is in some kind of trouble."

"Or maybe it's a trap to lure you into her clutches," said Aurora. "You must show the card to Inspector Cliff. Promise me, Rosie."

Rose nodded as the cab drew up outside Scotland Yard. As she stood up to leave she took another look at the picture on the front of the postcard. Then she said excitedly, "Do you remember that night back in the yard when Amy talked about Southend?" Aurora nodded. "Maybe this postcard is a clue as to where to find her. The question is, why is she so keen for me to find her?"

Aurora shrugged. "Ask Inspector Cliff. Maybe he'll know."

Rose wasn't at all confident that he would but she stepped down and walked into the police station, aware that Aurora was watching her every step of the way.

But when she got inside and asked for the inspector, saying it was in connection with the murder of Gandini and the disappearance of the Doomstone, she was told that he had been called out to a murder scene and nobody knew when he would be back. Rose guessed he must have gone to the river where Tobias's body had been found.

"You could speak to his assistant," said the policeman at the desk.

Rose shook her head. She had never seen Inspector Cliff with an assistant. She bit her lip, retrieved the postcard from her pocket and turned it over and over in her hand thinking hard. "Save me! For God's sake, help me." Maybe Amy was asking to be saved from herself? She walked out of Scotland Yard and headed towards Fenchurch Street Station. Rose was going to pay her first visit to the seaside. She walked quickly with her head down, so she didn't notice Inspector Cliff, hurrying up a side street towards the police station on his way back from the Pall Mall Theatre, where there had been a shocking discovery.

27

Rose sat alone in the wood-panelled train compartment with its sturdy overhead luggage racks. The almost empty steam train was shuddering as if eager to depart. It was not a day to go to the seaside. The air was brooding and the scorched city had an expectant air, as if waiting for the storm. With luck, and no delays, Rose felt confident that she could get to Southend and, if she was fortunate, find the cottages on the postcard, locate Amy and still get back to Southwark in time to change for Edward and Lydia's wedding. She was excited and nervous: was she about to uncover the mystery of the missing Doomstone and find out who had really killed Gandini and maybe Tobias Fraggles too?

It was unbearably hot in the train compartment,

even though she kept the sliding door to the corridor open, and the windows too. The whistle sounded. The train screeched. She put her head out of the window and, masked by the billows of smoke from the engine, she caught a glimpse of Billy Proctor running full tilt and just leaping into the final carriage, even as the train was pulling away. Rose's stomach lurched as if in sympathy with the train. Billy Proctor! What was he doing on the train? Was he in league with Amy too? Or could it be Billy Proctor that Amy was afraid of? But why? She suddenly wished that she had followed Aurora's advice and waited for Inspector Cliff, and told him everything she knew and suspected.

She stepped out into the corridor and made her way cautiously towards the next carriage. She could see Billy at the far end, working his way towards her, but he was so busy looking into every compartment that he didn't notice her. Who was he looking for? She didn't see how it could be her. Nobody knew she was going to Southend. But that didn't mean she wanted him to discover her on the train. She didn't trust him.

She peeped into the next carriage again. He was getting closer, systematically making his way through, looking into every compartment. She returned to her compartment, slid the door closed and climbed on to the banquette, then hauled herself up into the luggage rack. She lay quite still. As long as Billy didn't look upwards, but simply glanced into the compartment to see if anyone was sitting there, she might yet evade him. She held her breath. She saw him pass and his back disappearing down the corridor towards the front of the train. She heaved a sigh of relief and shifted her position slightly. Until they got to Southend this was as safe a place as any.

She remained undisturbed all the way and only scrambled down from the luggage rack as the train steamed into the station. When the stationmaster called out, "All change" she lingered in the compartment and watched as the few passengers walked down the platform. Billy Proctor stood by the exit, eyeing them closely, but as the last stragglers reached him he turned on his heel and left. Rose waited for another minute or two and then she stepped down from the train. At the exit she handed in her ticket to the stationmaster. She could see Billy's hunched back walking along the road, following a straggle of people who she assumed were all heading into town.

She pulled the postcard out of her pocket and showed it to the ticket collector.

"Do you know where I can find these cottages?" she asked.

"You'll find plenty of fishermen's cottages that look like them if you head that way." He pointed to a scraggy path across heathland. "Take that local short cut. It will bring you out on the seafront, then head round the bay."

Rose set off at a run. The sky glowered above her, angry and seething. A few huge drops of rain fell, bringing welcome relief from the still oppressive heat. From far away there was an ominous rumble. She hurried onwards. The path climbed a little higher and suddenly she got her first glimpse of the sea. It wasn't a sparkling blue as she had imagined, but grey and moody, as if something angry was bubbling in its depths, trying to get out. Rose shivered, and far out at sea there was a flash of lightning, cracking the sky apart.

Rose reached the seafront. She walked briskly along it, past the shops and boarding houses, heading north around the bay. The rain was falling faster and harder now, stinging as it hit her face. She was wearing only a thin dress and stockings and she was already soaked through. A vicious wind had whipped up from nowhere, and up ahead of her a woman was struggling to close a blue candy-striped awning that was resisting her and flapping wildly. Rose ran to help her and together they succeeded. There was a name written in gold lettering across the top of the window: Gandini's. Underneath in smaller words it said: Ice Creams of Distinction.

The woman pushed her into the shop with profuse thanks and offered her a towel.

"My husband normally does the awning but he's blind and gets disorientated in a storm, and he's got bad lungs and I didn't want him out. Can I get you a cup of tea to warm you?"

Rose shook her head and produced the damp postcard from her pocket. "Do you know where I'll find these cottages?"

"You're going the right way," said the woman kindly. "But they don't look so picturesque these days. Some of them are abandoned. It's too isolated out there for most, and the rocks are treacherous for the fishing boats. Looking for anyone in particular?"

"A girl. Amy. About my age. Sandy-coloured hair. Legs like a foal. Gooseberry-green eyes. I think she might be staying in one of the cottages."

The woman smiled. "Oh, you mean Amelia. Lovely girl. Her and her dad rent one of the cottages from us; it used to belong to my mother. My husband has known Amelia's dad since he was just a boy. I hadn't seen them for a couple of years – they were in America – but the rent was still being paid regular as clockwork, and they asked me to go up and air the place every week. Then a few months ago they came back for a couple of weekends. Then nothing again, and then Amelia turned up out of the blue really late at night two days ago, banging on the door and asking for the key. Must have come on the last train from London. I asked about her father and she burst into tears and closed up like an oyster. I could see something was wrong. I'd say she was frightened. I tried to comfort her but she wouldn't let me near, poor little lamb."

"Have you seen her since?" asked Rose.

"Yes, early yesterday morning, here in the town buying a newspaper. She was clearly upset."

So, thought Rose to herself, Amy – or maybe

she should call her Amelia – had fled here as soon as she had killed her father, and she must have found out about Effie standing trial from the paper. The fact that the woman was saying the girl was upset made her feel more comfortable. Aurora had warned her that the note might be a trap, but maybe Amy simply wanted to make a confession and that's why she had lured her here. The woman was telling her that she needed to look for a pink-painted cottage with yellow muslin curtains at the end of the row. Rose thanked her and went to leave. At the door she turned.

"Have you ever heard of a magician with your name, Gandini?"

The woman shook her head. "No, not related to us." Clearly, unlike Amy – or Amelia – the woman hadn't been reading the newspapers and knew nothing of the magician's sensational murder and Effie's trial. "I always thought Amelia and her dad could have gone on the stage. They are that good at doing conjuring tricks. Sometimes do them in the shop to entertain my little 'uns. I told her dad they should set up as a magician and his assistant, but he said that Amelia was far too good to be anyone's assistant. They are a lovely pair. He's one of nature's true gentlemen. I've always thought it a pity that he has no wife. He'd make some woman very happy."

"Thank you for your help," said Rose.

For a moment she hesitated, wondering whether she should return to London and tell the inspector what she had discovered. But then she remembered Billy Proctor's presence on the train. Could it have been Proctor who killed Gandini? Maybe on Amy's behalf? He'd had the opportunity. Perhaps the apparently butter-fingered Proctor had conjuring skills too? He had been present when Lydia had had the Doomstone taken from around her neck. Or maybe Amy had nothing to do with killing her father, and that's why she was scared. Perhaps it had been Amy that Billy Proctor had been looking for on the train. She'd never forgive herself if at this very moment he was attacking Amy and she didn't try to intervene.

She began to run, only stopping when she reached the cottages set back from the shoreline. There was no smoke coming from any of the chimneys, and one of them was partly boarded up. It was a desolate place, made all the more lonely by the roar of the sea and the hurling rain. The sky split again, followed by a boom of thunder so loud it sounded as if Doomsday had arrived. The edges of the clouds were laced black, as if they had all been singed. Rose walked up to the door of the pink cottage and knocked loudly. There was no answer. She knocked again. Then she put her hand on the door handle and turned it. The door was unlocked. She gave it a gentle push. It swung partially open.

Cautiously she stepped through the door, straight into a small parlour. On one side of the room was a narrow staircase leading to the upper floor of the little house; on the other a door, which Rose guessed led to a scullery at the back of the house. The parlour was simply furnished with a sofa, a small wooden table and two chairs. There was also a sideboard and on it sat something blue and sparkling: the Doomstone! It was here! Excited, she took another step forward, when suddenly she felt a blow to the back of her skull. Her head seared with pain. Her knees crumpled and she collapsed to the floor.

28

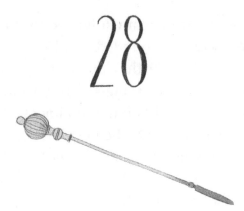

"Rose! Rose! Please wake up."

Rose opened her eyes to see Amy's pale, haunted face. She touched her head and winced. Amy was still holding the poker she had used to hit Rose. But Rose had to admit that Amy didn't look like a ruthless, cold-blooded murderer who had dispatched her father and was now planning to finish her off. She looked hopeless and unhappy. Amy helped Rose to her feet and led her over to the sofa. Rose sank into it, still eyeing Amy warily.

"Oh, Rose, I'm so sorry about your head. Is it all right? I thought you were someone else, come to kill me."

"Billy Proctor?" asked Rose, feeling the tender

spot on her head. Fortunately the skin wasn't broken.

Amy shook her head. "Billy Proctor? Why would I hit Campion's barman over the head, and what reason would he have to want to kill me?"

"Because he's here in Southend."

Amy looked even more puzzled. "It must just be an odd coincidence."

"I don't know," said Rose. "I got the distinct feeling that he was looking for someone. I assumed it was you. I thought perhaps the two of you were in league together and that he killed your father on your instructions. Gandini was your father, wasn't he?"

Amy nodded and burst into noisy tears. "I'd never have killed my father. I loved him. He was the kindest of men." She stared at Rose, looking horrified. "Is that what you think, Rose? That I'm a heartless murderess who orders people to kill for me?"

"To be honest, Amy – or should I say Melly or Amelia – I don't know what to think. All I know is that Effie is locked up for life in Holloway Prison for killing your father, and I'd stake my life she didn't do it. I also know that everyone thinks that you're dead, and quite clearly you're very much alive. If that's not suspicious I don't know what is. And you put a note in my pocket saying that you needed saving, and a significant clue as to where to find you."

Amy smiled. "That was a spur-of-the moment decision when I saw you outside the court. I only had a second to scrawl it. I was nervous that you wouldn't work it out, but I thought you would because you're so clever, Rose. In fact, when I faked my death, you were the only person I was worried would think it odd that I had left my dress on the steps before jumping into the river. I doubted Inspector Cliff would notice."

"I told the inspector how strange I thought it was," said Rose. "And I know you saw Edward that night. He told Aurora and me that he spotted you on the Devil's Steps."

"Yes," said Amy. "I almost fell into the river in shock when he turned up in Rotherhithe on the night I was supposed to be faking my suicide. It was such bad luck. He's a blind fool, just like my dad, but I felt really terrible that I was deceiving him so monstrously. I was worried that dozy inspector would arrest him for killing me, because I was sure that Edward would tell him he'd been there when my disappearance became public. I felt bad about sending him on a wild goose chase by saying I'd seen Jem heading towards Campion's, particularly when I heard the awful thing that happened to Jem. Is he any better?"

Rose nodded. "Doing surprisingly well. Lottie says there's every chance he'll make a full recovery. But tell me, Amy – what happened after Edward left you on the steps?"

"I was wearing boy's clothes under my dress, so as soon as he'd gone and I was certain nobody was around, I slipped out of my dress, put up my hair under a cap and walked away, leaving my dress folded on the steps."

Rose remembered the boy that Edward reported seeing walking along the river path after he had doubled-back to the steps. That must have been Amy.

"So you faked your own death. But why? And you have yet to convince me that you didn't kill your own father – it's quite clear that you did steal the Doomstone," said Rose, nodding towards the jewel on the sideboard.

Amy laughed. "Oh, Rose, don't be silly, that's not the Doomstone. It's just a Christmas tree bauble. But it's very precious to me. It's a memento of freedom – of the first Christmas my father and I spent alone together after we escaped from the Duchess."

"The Duchess?" Rose leaned forward in excitement. "Who exactly are you and your father?"

"We are Paul and Amelia Bray. My grandmother is Ruth Bray, known as the Duchess. She is currently locked up in Holloway Prison, where I hope and pray she will stay until she dies. She is as ruthless as a stiletto. My father was her son, known for many years as the Gentleman Dipper. From a boy he hated his life in the criminal underworld. But there was no escaping the Duchess. If you crossed her, you paid. Even if you were family. My mother ended up dead in the Regent's Canal when I was seven, for telling the Duchess that she was evil and she wanted out. My father's younger sister, a lovely woman with dreams of being an actress, suffered a similar fate. After that, my father waited patiently and planned. He knew that if he left with me the Duchess would do everything in her power to take her revenge. He had to get as far away as he could from her, and he needed a way to earn an honest living in a place where we would be safe.

"The honest living was stage magic. He realised that conjuring is just another form of prigging and conning – except, for one, you get paid and applauded, and for the other, you steal and risk ending up in the clink. Eventually, just before the Duchess was about to get me started as a prigger on the streets, we managed to escape and went to America, where my father rechristened himself Gandini and started working the halls there as a magician. He took the name because the Gandini family had been so kind to him when he was a boy – kinder than his own mother, who saw all goodness as a weakness. And my dad always loved a penny lick. In America we were beyond the reach of the Duchess. But then my father heard that the Duchess had been arrested and convicted with a life sentence, and so he decided we should return."

"So," said Rose excitedly, "it must be somebody working for the Duchess who killed your father."

Amy shook her head. "No! Although my father was always nervous about her reach, I doubt that even the Duchess could organise my father's murder from Holloway Prison. I'm pretty safe from her malevolence as long as she's inside. There is little honour among thieves. Without her son to keep the family firm going, her power probably evaporated as soon as she was banged up."

"So when you hit me over the head with the poker, who did you think had come to kill you?"

"Haven't you worked it out? Lydia, of course. It was Lydia who stole the Doomstone from around her own neck and then killed my father. She was my father's assistant before she became his wife."

Rose's eyes bulged. "Lydia is Gandini's wife?"

"Well, technically," said Amy bitterly. "I suppose she is now his widow."

29

The girls were sitting side by side on the sofa.

"My father met Lydia in America. He was looking for a magician's assistant and she applied. She was an unsuccessful actress, down on her luck. Papa could see her potential – but even if she had been hamfisted he would have employed Lydia. It was love at first sight for him. He adored her. He taught her everything he knew, and I have to admit she learned quickly.

"The act was doing well. It wasn't an easy life, but there was more than enough money, and as the halls my father played got bigger, so did the financial rewards. Papa was very homesick – he longed to return to England and settle quietly here in Southend, where he had spent his holidays as a boy before the Duchess made him start learning his trade as a pickpocket and conman. But that was impossible, because the Duchess would hunt him down. In America he was making a decent living, and doing it honestly, and that made him feel good. He proposed to Lydia and she accepted. I don't think she loved him, but I like to think she was fond of him, and at that point in her life she was grateful for some security. My father would do anything to please her, so marriage was an agreeable prospect."

"But it didn't last?" asked Rose.

Amy shook her head. "It might have done if we'd stayed in the backwaters, but as the act got more successful we moved to bigger cities, where Lydia's eyes were opened to real wealth. She became more and more discontented. She had the love of my father and more than enough money, but as Lydia saw how some other people lived she was eaten up with envy. She didn't just want a good life; she wanted a charmed life. And she realised she had the opportunity to get it. Men buzzed around Lydia.

"After we'd been in New York for a few weeks she disappeared. She left a note for Papa, speaking of her regret but saying that there was a big world out there, that she was still young and she wanted to discover it. He was heartbroken – utterly crushed. He took to his bed for days. Even though by then he knew full well what Lydia was like, he still adored her. He only saw the best in her. She was like a drug to him. He kept hoping that she would return, and when she didn't, it was as if a light had gone out inside him. The homesickness got worse, and he talked more and more about returning to England, despite the danger from the Duchess. Something else happened too. He developed terrible stage fright. It was as if Lydia leaving had knocked his confidence in every way. The run-up to every performance started to become a terror for him. But he had no choice. Conning or conjuring were the only things he knew. He dreamed of giving up the stage and coming to live here permanently. He had been secretly renting the cottage from the Gandini family for years, starting shortly after my mother was murdered. It was a bolthole away from the Duchess's world."

"Tell me about coming back to England," said Rose.

"News reached us that the Duchess had been banged up in Holloway for life. Papa decided that we should return home. The plan was to perform in England for a short while and then come here to Southend and live quietly. He negotiated a share in the Gandini ice cream shop in preparation for that time – the Gandinis are getting elderly and need help. He wanted me to stay in Southend as soon as we returned. He was very cautious, concerned that if any of the Duchess's old cronies were looking for us, they would be looking for a father and daughter together. But I didn't like being here on my own. It's too isolated. And then one night he was performing at a suburban hall, when who should turn up like a bad penny?"

"Lydia," breathed Rose.

Amy nodded. "Yes, on the arm of Stratford-Mark. She returned alone the next day. My father was thrilled. He was a clever man, but always a fool when it came to Lydia. He thought that this was his second chance with her, and she gave him every indication that was the case. She's a sly one, Lydia. She knows how to flatter a man."

Rose suddenly thought about Tobias Fraggles floating sightless in the Thames with a slit throat. Lydia must have charmed him into lying in court and then dispatched him when he had served his purpose.

"When Lydia proposed I work for her as a dresser, Papa jumped at the idea. It kept both Lydia and me close to him, but in my case not close enough that it might attract attention. What he didn't know was that it was all part of Lydia's plan to steal the Doomstone from around her own neck. She was in league with Stratford-Mark – he has terrible debts and would stoop to anything to save his theatre. They made an agreement. Stratford-Mark had the connections to provide the opportunity for Lydia to wear the diamond, and the means for its disposal if Lydia would do the deed. Lydia was skilled at conjuring, and she knew that a magic act, during which the audience's attention is diverted, would be the perfect opportunity for her to steal the Star of the Sea. Better still, who would ever imagine that Lydia had stolen the diamond from around her own neck? It could have been taken at the Alhambra or somewhere else, but it was at Campion's. It was Lydia who encouraged my father to approach Campion's. She said that she had heard that it was small and friendly and that it might suit my father, particularly because of his issues with stage fright, and he thought that it wasn't high profile enough to attract attention from the police or any of the Duchess's former cronies.

"Of course, on the night the Doomstone went missing, my father and I realised that Lydia's suggestion of Campion's had all been a set-up. She and Stratford-Mark knew of Edward's strong connection with the place and used it to their advantage, to make it seem as if the visit there was utterly unplanned and spontaneous."

Rose frowned. "So you and your father had nothing to do with the disappearance of the Doomstone?"

"Of course not," said Amy indignantly. "Papa had turned his back forever on a life of crime. He wouldn't have gone back to it, not even for Lydia. He was furious when he realised what she had done, incandescent with rage. He felt that he had been a dupe and that she had endangered him and me too. He had me change lodgings immediately, just in case."

"So why didn't he tell the police?"

Amy shrugged. "Two reasons. He still loved Lydia too much to put her behind bars for life, and he was worried about his own situation. Here in England he not only feared the possible threat of the Duchess, but also the much more substantial threat of the police. He had done some things in his past of which he was very ashamed. Unlike the Duchess, he never killed anybody but he had robbed and conned. He would still be wanted for those crimes. The second the Doomstone went missing he knew that Lydia was the only person who could possibly be responsible, but when it turned out that Inspector Cliff was present at Campion's on that night he became worried. He thought it less likely that the inspector knew in advance about Lydia and Stratford-Mark's plot to steal the Doomstone, and far more probable that the inspector was on his trail, having made a connection between Paul Bray and Gandini. He was furious with Lydia for putting his position in such jeopardy. But he decided that staying put was the safest option. If he fled it would look like guilt, and he'd be on the run for the rest of his life, and if arrested he'd get done for stealing the Doomstone on top of everything else. And if he told the inspector that he knew that Lydia had stolen the Doomstone from around her own neck, he'd be betraying the woman he still loved.

"It was an impossible position and of course

Lydia played on it, insisting that her relationship with Edward was simply faked for the purpose of stealing the Doomstone, and hinting that my father was the great love of her life. As soon as all the fuss died down, she claimed that she would be returning to his arms. Of course, I could see from spending time with Lydia and Edward every day that Papa was a fool to believe a word, but he was blindsided by love. He didn't like it when I told him he was being a dupe again.

"So when the heat was on and it looked as if the inspector might be about to make an arrest, he came up with the plan for me to fake my own death. He thought that if everyone believed that I was the culprit, and the Doomstone was at the bottom of the river, the inspector would close the investigation – perhaps even lose interest in my father. Of course, Lydia was thrilled by the plan – so thrilled that she told my father she regretted her terrible mistake in stealing the Doomstone, and promised him that as soon as the fuss faded away she would return to live with him in Southend.

"I knew that would never happen. Can you imagine Lydia living here? In any case, she's not just in love with Edward – it's more like an obsession. I don't know what happened next, but I assume my father must have finally realised, or been told by somebody, that Lydia was lying to him, and confronted her in some fashion, and so she killed him and framed Effie.

"As soon as I heard that he'd been killed, I knew that Lydia would come looking for me next. That's why I went to the court, in the hope that I'd be able to find Thomas or Edward and confess all. I saw you outside and hoped you'd help. I was anxious how you'd react because you thought I was dead. But there was no choice. Then, as I approached you, I saw Lydia with Edward in the distance looming from the other crowd. It was too risky. So I scribbled the note and stuffed it in your pocket."

Rose nodded. It was all falling into place. Effie had casually told Gandini just before the show about Lydia and Edward's forthcoming nuptials, and Rose hadn't misheard when she had thought that she had heard Gandini say softly to Lydia, "I know. I'll stop it," during the bullet trick. Those words had sealed his fate. Lydia would know that the only way she could ensure his silence was to kill him.

"So," said Rose excitedly. "Lydia killed

Gandini, setting it up to make it look as if Effie was responsible with the pearl bullet and the faked note. Then, just to make sure that Effie took the blame, she got Tobias to testify against Effie and killed him to ensure his silence. You've good reason to be worried that Lydia will come for you next."

"Yes," said a voice behind them. "She does. And sadly so do you."

They spun round. Lydia was standing behind them, pointing a pistol. She looked very pale and unusually dishevelled. She must have entered the house through the back door in the scullery, and the noise of the storm meant that they hadn't heard her. "It's such a pity that I can't risk you telling anyone else."

30

"That should do the job," said Lydia calmly, as she secured the final knot that bound both girls together around the waist. She stood back and once again rubbed her hands together in a nervous gesture, as if trying to clean them of a stain. They were upstairs in the tiny back bedroom of the cottage. Rose and Amy had their hands and feet tied together. Lydia had produced twine from her bag and ordered Amy at gunpoint to bind Rose's hands and feet, and when Amy had deliberately made a hash of it, Lydia had held the pistol to Amy's head with such a wild look in her eye that Rose had said quietly, "Do it properly, Amy."

Amy obliged, tying the knots tightly. Once Rose was immobilised on the floor, Lydia had picked up a vase and smashed it over Amy's head, stunning the girl so that she could quickly secure her hands and feet. Now the two girls were lying side by side on the bed, each tied to one of the bedposts at the top. Lydia had closed the small window in the bedroom and the shutters too. Even so, the noise from the thunderstorm outside was still deafening. The rain was hitting the roof tiles like bullets, every clap of thunder sounding like an explosion. The storm was clearly right overhead.

"Lydia," said Rose urgently. "You don't have to do this. Just let us go. We won't tell anyone. You could just disappear."

"Disappear?" said Lydia, sounding surprised. "I have no intention of disappearing on my wedding day. I will be at the church to marry Edward in a few hours, as arranged. I'm doing all this for him. We love each other, and nothing must ever get in the way of that. My life changed the moment I set eyes on Edward. That night will be forever engraved upon my heart.

"Gandini had told me he would be performing at Campion's that week, and I immediately realised that it was the perfect cover for me to steal the Doomstone. All Stratford-Mark had to do was introduce me to Edward after the first night of *Hamlet*. It was perfect. I was supposed to feign an interest in Edward. In front of a whole roomful of witnesses, the spur-of-the-moment decision to go to Campion's would be made. Once there, I would steal the diamond under cover of Gandini's performance, and keep it until I could pass it on to Stratford-Mark, who would hide it at the theatre until it was safe to dispose of it. I was to get half of the proceeds. Stratford-Mark could clear his debts and be set up for life. But what I hadn't calculated was that I would fall in love with Edward. As soon as I saw him I was lost. Quite lost. Even if he had been a pauper I would have followed him to the ends of the earth. My heart was no longer my own. It was his."

She looked at Amy sorrowfully.

"Just as your poor father couldn't escape his past, I couldn't stop what I had put in motion. The ridiculous thing is that the moment I met Edward there was no longer any need for me to commit the theft. Love, wealth and position were all within my grasp. As soon as I had stolen the Doomstone I regretted it deeply

– particularly when it so quickly became apparent to me that Edward felt as passionately about me as I felt about him. I'd have done anything to turn back the clock. The only thing that now mattered was our happiness together, and of course the investigation into the Doomstone's disappearance kept threatening that. I wish I had never touched the silly stone. Meeting Edward was my redemption. Alas it came too late."

Once again she was rubbing her hands together in an agitated fashion.

"I knew that I could count on your father's love to keep silent about my involvement, as long as he thought that I might return to him. So I wanted to keep my forthcoming marriage to Edward a secret as long as possible. I doubted that even his love would extend to my marrying another man, or that he would countenance bigamy, so although I really didn't wish him any harm, I knew that I would have to deal with him sooner rather than later. It became apparent on the evening of the bullet trick that the moment had come, and that the circumstances favoured me: by implicating Effie, I could escape all suspicion. Gandini helped with his final fateful words. To make quite sure of Effie's conviction I got Tobias Fraggles to testify, and then of course I had to deal with him. And as soon as I spotted you outside the court, Amy, I knew I would have to deal with you too. And now with you too, Rose. I've no choice. I'm really very sorry."

She looked genuinely sad.

"Over the last few days I've begun to feel as if the Doomstone has cursed me in a very particular way." She looked distant for a moment and whispered, "The blood. There has been so much blood." She rubbed her hands together. "These hands will never be clean." She smiled sorrowfully and said, "Forgive me, girls. I really am very sorry."

Then she removed the key from the door and left the room, shutting the door behind her. They heard the key turn in the lock and Lydia's footsteps on the stairs. A few moments later, in a lull in the storm, the front door banged. The girls looked at each other, puzzled. They had both thought that Lydia was going to shoot them before she left.

"Come on," said Rose. "Let's get these knots undone. Try using your teeth." For a few minutes they struggled in silence, making very little headway.

Then Rose stopped and sniffed. The smell was unmistakeable. Fire! Lydia had set the cottage on fire. Smoke began to creep under the door of the bedroom, a silent, deadly puddle. Rose's mind was racing. Their deaths would most likely look like an accident, the cottage struck by lightning and burned to the ground with them in it. There was a roll of thunder from outside. The smoke was getting thicker. There was a crackle from the flames licking at the door. Lydia had set the fire burning on the staircase, so even if they had succeeded in breaking their bonds they would be trapped. Rose twisted on the bed. The floorboards of the bedroom seemed to be creaking as if in pain. It was getting unbearably hot. Flames were dancing across the floor, moving closer to the bed. A fallen bolster caught a flame with a popping sound. Amy's eyes were glazed with fear. There was a roar of flame as the door caved in and the girls were hit by a wave of heat, and could see the inferno moving towards them like a wall. Amy screamed. There was a clap of thunder and under it, Rose heard the smashing of glass and the sound of an axe on wood. There was a splintering, cracking noise and suddenly the shutters burst open. Billy Proctor appeared, illuminated by lightning so it seemed as if the outline of his body was lit up and in shock. He knocked the rest of the glass out of the window and then clambered through into the room. He quickly cut the girls loose from the bedpost with the axe, untied Rose's hands and feet, and together they untied Amy. A river of flame was running around the edge of the room, tonguing the chest of drawers, whose white paint was melting. As soon as the last knot was untied, Billy pushed them to the window, all three coughing and spluttering. Rose's throat felt as if it were on fire; her eyes watered and stung. One by one they began to climb down the rickety ladder. Billy followed last, and had just reached the bottom when there was a terrible sound, as if the entire cottage was groaning to itself.

"Run!" he shouted, the first word that anyone had uttered since his miraculous appearance at the window. They dashed to the end of the garden and turned back towards the cottage as a fork of lightning illuminated the roof. There was a thunderclap so mighty that it made their ears hurt, and then the entire building seemed to shriek in agony, as it lurched and started to fall in upon itself.

"Lucky escape," said Billy drily, surveying the inferno. He gave Amy a long look. "Looks like you've got a knack of cheating death. Like a cat with nine lives."

"Thanks for the rescue," said Rose, wiping dirt and smoke out of her eyes. "But we're in a bit of a hurry. We need to get to the station. We've got a wedding to stop."

"Yes, we need to hurry. I saw Lydia heading across the heath for the station," said Billy. "I was going to go after her, when I saw the smoke and thought I'd better investigate. I'm glad I did. I don't know how it all fits together, but would I be right in assuming that Amy here is Amelia, daughter of Paul Bray, otherwise known as the magician Gandini, and that it was Lydia who tried to murder you?"

Rose and Amy nodded. "There's no time to waste explaining now. We'll tell all when we're on the London train," said Rose, setting off at a run. Billy nodded his agreement. "Just one question," added Rose as she sprinted. "What are you doing in Southend, and who are you?

If there's one thing I'm quite certain of it's that you are definitely not a barman by trade."

Billy grinned. "I kept waiting for you to call me out, Rose. It was obvious you had your suspicions about me from the start. And you were right. Until I got the job at Campion's I'd never been behind a bar in my life. I'm a policeman. I'm Inspector Cliff's assistant. I was sent to Campion's to keep an eye on the magician Gandini, who we had our suspicions was really Paul Bray, the Gentleman Dipper. But then the Doomstone went missing and that completely changed the nature of the investigation."

Rose recalled the times she had seen Billy outside Holloway Prison. Julia Devonish had been telling the truth when she said that Billy had been seeing the Duchess. She must have known he was a policeman planted at Campion's.

They hurried on, lashed by rain and at the mercy of the wind, but they arrived at the station just in time to see the train steaming out. There wasn't another one for half an hour.

"I'll telegraph to the Yard and get Inspector Cliff and his officers to meet the train and arrest Lydia for your attempted murder," said Billy.

But when he spoke to the stationmaster he

was told that the storm had brought down the lines and that wouldn't be possible. There was nothing to do but wait for the eight o'clock train.

"If the train makes it here," said Billy darkly.

"It's got to come," said Rose desperately, "or Edward will end up married to a murderess."

"You'd better tell me everything you know while we wait," said Billy.

"How did you know to come to Southend?"

"You have Aurora to thank for that. She turned up at Scotland Yard, asking for the inspector. He had been at the Pall Mall. Stratford-Mark had been found dead there. Looked like a suicide. There was even a note." He shook his head. "But the inspector had his doubts."

"Lydia's doing," said Amy bitterly. "Another one of her victims."

Billy nodded. "Just as you two would have been if Aurora hadn't decided to return to the Yard to check that you had spoken to the inspector as promised. She got there just as he arrived back. The man at the desk told us that somebody fitting your description had been asking for the inspector, and had left when told he was out. Aurora guessed you had gone to Southend in search of Amy, and told us all about the postcard and what had happened outside the court. The inspector had never quite believed that Amy was dead, so he dispatched me. I looked for you on the train."

"I know," said Rose. "I hid. I thought maybe you were in league with Amy. Amy, you'd better tell Billy everything you told me about Lydia."

Amy did so, and by the time the train arrived to take them to London, Billy knew the whole sad history of Lydia and Gandini and had been able to fill them in on what he and the inspector already knew.

The train suffered further delays and so by the time they arrived at Fenchurch Street the station clock read a quarter to ten. Billy told them to go ahead. He would send a message to Scotland Yard to get the police to go to St Olave's before following them.

"We'll never make it to St Olave's in time," said Rose desperately, and it looked as though she was going to be right – the terrible weather meant that there wasn't a hansom in sight. At last they found one and it set off towards Southwark, moving slowly through the murky night, with the rain drumming on the top of the cab so loudly that it was impossible to hear each other speak. The side roads had turned to mud and were treacherous, made slippery with grease and water so that the horses could get little grip.

"We're going to be too late," said Rose despairingly. The city clock struck ten p.m. long before they reached London Bridge. They clattered on to the bridge and the tower of St Olave's came into view through the mist. They trundled on as a flash of lightning split the sky, lighting up the river eerily. The thunder that followed was so loud that the horses reared, and the carriage lurched into the gutter, one of the wheels buckling. They were stuck. Rose flung some coins at Amy to give to the cab driver, leapt from the carriage and began running across the bridge, the rain driving into her face like needles. At the south side of the bridge the road was completely blocked by an overturned cart. A horse was loose, spooked by the thunder and lightning. Rose didn't stop. She turned left at the end of the bridge and tore along the riverbank. Her breath was coming in ragged gasps, her throat felt raw with the exertion and she was soaked through, her face streaked with soot. She raced through the churchyard, glimpsed the candles glimmering inside the church windows and ran up the path to the church's great door. She turned the iron ring handles and flung the great doors open. Through the carved wooden screen in front, she could see Edward and Lydia standing at the altar with their backs to her. The priest had his nose buried in his book.

"If anyone knows of any impediment—"

"Stop! I do!" shouted Rose, and she raced up the aisle. Everyone turned to look at her. Water and sweat and soot were running down her face and she knew she looked quite mad. Edward stepped backwards in astonishment. Aurora had stood up and was staring at Rose, white-faced. Lydia took a closer step towards Edward, as if seeking sanctuary behind him. Rose pointed her finger at Lydia.

"I don't know if it's a legal impediment. But you can't marry her, Edward. She was married to Gandini and she killed him. And she tried to kill Amy and me too. And she probably killed Tobias Fraggles, and maybe Stratford-Mark too."

Everyone began to talk at once. Lydia gave a harsh laugh. "The child's quite mad. Just look at the state of her! She's telling lies, wicked lies."

"No, she's not," shouted Amy, who had arrived at the church looking quite as dishevelled and drowned as Rose.

A murmur of consternation went up in the church with the unexpected appearance of Amy. Edward took another step backwards as if he'd seen a ghost. Thomas put his hand to his mouth in astonishment.

"Lydia stole the Doomstone from around her own neck, and she killed my father when he discovered that she was planning to marry Edward, even though she was still married to him."

"It's true, Edward," said Rose quietly.

"Edward..." said Lydia pleadingly. "It's just childish..." She stuttered to a halt. Edward was looking at her as if he was seeing her for the very first time. He put his head to one side.

"Lydia?" he said questioningly. "I think you have some explaining to do."

"She does," said another voice, and Inspector Cliff, Billy Proctor and several other policemen appeared at the end of the aisle. "Lydia Bray, sometimes known as Lydia Duchamps, I'm arresting you for the theft of the Doomstone, the murder of Paul Bray, otherwise known as Mr

Gandini, and for the attempted murder of Rose Campion and Amelia Bray. Further charges will follow."

"It's all some silly mistake," blustered Lydia, but she faltered as she saw the way that everyone was looking at her with a mixture of astonishment and distaste. "Edward," she said pleadingly, and faltered to a stop. Edward was staring at her as if she was a stranger – one repulsive to him at that. Inspector Cliff was bearing down on her, handcuffs ready. Lydia didn't wait – she gathered her short train under one arm, darted towards a small wooden door to her left and ran through it, kicking it shut behind her.

Amy, quicker off the mark than the others, was after her with no hesitation. She flung the door open again, revealing a stone spiral staircase, and chased up after Lydia, closely followed by Rose. Rose knew that Lydia had made a mistake: the staircase led nowhere but the top of the bell tower. Lydia was going to be trapped. Rose could hear Amy ahead, and the sound of feet behind her. Up ahead, another door banged. Lydia must have reached the bell tower. There was nowhere for her to go but the roof. Rose reached the small door at the top of the staircase and burst through it. She was in the bell tower. Lydia was already disappearing through a trapdoor at the top of a ladder clamped to the wall. Amy was close behind Lydia. Rose clambered on to the bottom of the ladder as Amy's feet disappeared above her. Rose scrambled up as fast as she could and emerged on to the roof of the tower to find Lydia with her arm around Amy's neck, pointing a pistol at her head. Lydia had a look of desperation that Rose had seen once before, in the eyes of a mad dog that had been chased through the streets and cornered in an alleyway.

Rose could almost feel the threatening metal barrel of the pistol, as if it was being held against her own temple. The inspector, Billy, Edward and the others had reached the top of the tower and Rose sensed them behind her, weighing up the situation and holding their breath. There was a flash of lightning that illuminated everyone, so they resembled startled ghosts. Rose realised how dangerously exposed they were up on the church roof in the middle of a raging storm.

"Lydia, put down the gun. Let Amy go," said Edward, and he moved next to Rose.

"Do as he says, Lydia. You can't escape from

here," said the inspector, and he put out his hand for the gun and took a step closer.

"Stay where you are," shouted Lydia, "or she gets it in the head." She gave a little laugh. "What's one more?" She looked distracted. "There has been so much blood."

Rose was suddenly reminded of Lady Macbeth, driven mad by all the slaughter she had instigated. She wondered whether Lydia had lost her mind. The inspector was once again talking in a low voice to Lydia.

"Let the girl go. We can work something out, Lydia." There was another flash, and a clap of thunder as loud as judgement day. It rumbled on and on, as if the entrails of the city itself were groaning. Lydia was waving the gun around and talking to herself. Amy whimpered. The inspector took a step towards Lydia and she fired the gun, the bullet narrowly missing his right ear.

"I will kill the girl. Blood will have blood," said Lydia.

Rose suddenly had an idea. Lydia was past reason, but perhaps she was still in touch with her emotions. She whispered something to Edward, who nodded and then turned his gaze to Lydia and looked at her as if she and he were the only two people present.

He said softly, "Lydia. My love! Listen to me. You and me. That's all that matters. You know how much you mean to me."

Lydia looked at him. For a moment there was a hint of suspicion in her gaze, but when she saw the sincerity in his face it melted away. It was suddenly as if Lydia was lit from within, looking as beautiful and luminous as she had on that first evening, when they had glimpsed her at the Pall Mall wearing the Star of the Sea.

"Edward," she sighed softly. "You still love me?" Edward nodded. "Despite everything you still want to marry me?"

Edward's back was full of tension, but he said gently, "Of course, my love. You know I'd do anything for you."

Lydia gazed at him lovingly. "I'd do anything for you, Edward."

"I know, Lydia. That's why I'm asking you to let Amy go. Please – do it for me, my love. There has been enough blood spilled."

"Yes," whispered Lydia. "Blood will have blood. I'm very tired, Edward. I'm so very tired. The old man, Stratford-Mark, had so much blood in him. I want it to stop."

"I know, my love," said Edward. "Let me help you. We'll stop it together. Side by side."

He moved up very close to her, and Lydia dropped the hand with the gun in it to her side in a gesture of defeat. Rose sensed the inspector was going to move forward and she motioned for him to stop. There was another flash of lightning followed by more thunder. Amy began to edge away, but Lydia seemed to have entirely forgotten her. Rain was running like tears down Lydia's and Edward's faces as they gazed intensely at each other, her eyes lost in his and his lost in hers.

"Will you hand the gun to me, my love?" asked Edward. Lydia smiled and looked deeper still into his eyes. She held the gun out, and he took it and kissed her hand.

"Thank you, Lydia. Thank you, my love." For a moment he gazed down at her, and she looked up at him, and it felt as if the world had stopped moving and they were the only two people on earth. He moved so that he was now standing alongside, but still not touching her. He held out his arm and gave a gallant little bow.

"Will you take my arm, m'lady?"

Lydia smiled sweetly and dropped a little curtsy.

"I will, m'lud." She raised her arm so he could hook his around hers, and as she did so there was a bright flash and an almighty bang. A look of astonishment passed across Lydia's face and she fell to the ground, her body charred and smoking. She had taken the full force of a lightning strike. There was a moment of shocked silence, and then Edward crumpled and began to weep, very quietly at first, and then like a dog howling at the moon.

31

Afterwards

Rose, Aurora, Thomas, Edward and Amy were waiting in the yard of Holloway Prison. Rose gazed up at the forbidding walls and shivered. The iron door at the end of the yard opened and Effie appeared, a tiny hunched figure. She saw them all and her face lit up like the sun on a summer's morning. They all flung themselves towards her and she disappeared under their hugs. As they walked towards the gatehouse, chatting away, the inspector and Julia Devonish came to greet them, both of them beaming. The inspector took Effie's hand.

"My apologies. I hope you can forgive me for all my stupidity. I was blind, quite blind to the truth."

Effie smiled graciously. "It don't matter. It's

over now." She gazed at the prison walls and muttered fiercely, "I ain't never going back in there." Then she winked at Julia. "I hope you don't mind me saying, ma'am, but the food is rubbish. I can't wait to get a Campion's bloater down my throat."

Julia smiled. "The inspector has more news."

The inspector nodded and turned to Rose. "I owe you thanks, Rose Campion. We may never have recovered the Star of the Sea if it were not for you. We turned the Pall Mall upside down in vain, until you suggested that we take a look at the chandeliers, and there it was in plain sight, hidden amid the other pieces of coloured glass. It would still be there, maybe for eternity, if it was not for you."

"If there is one thing I've learned over the last few weeks," said Rose, "it's that the best place to hide something is in plain view. You never notice what is staring you in the face."

"Well, thank you." He turned to Thomas. "Of course Campion's can reopen tonight if you wish. My apologies for the inconvenience, and if I can ever be of any service—"

"Maybe you can," said Rose quickly. She looked at Thomas, who nodded. "It's about my mother. I was stolen from her when I was just a baby. Thomas found me, and he has been the best father any girl could ever hope to have, but I do so feel the lack of a mother, and I can't bear to think that maybe she's out there somewhere too, feeling the lack of me. We've been looking for her, and we've asked the police to help over and over, but so far they don't seem to be trying very hard. Do you think you could look into it when you don't have any murders to investigate?"

"Of course," said the inspector, "Billy and I will be on to it first thing in the morning. We will make it a priority. It is the very least we can do."

He and Julia took their leave.

"Do you really think he'll be able to help?" asked Aurora.

"You never know," said Thomas. "Anything is worth a try."

"It is," said Rose. "I'm sure that the inspector will do his best." She paused wickedly. "But as we all know, the inspector's best is not very good."

They all burst out laughing. Two carriages were waiting for them outside the prison.

"We'll drop you off at Fenchurch Street, Amy," said Thomas. "Are you sure you don't want any of us to come to Southend with you?"

Amy shook her head. "Mrs Gandini said she would meet me at the station. She said I can start work this afternoon in the shop. I'm so looking forward to it, learning how to make ice cream properly. Anyway, Rose, Rory and Effie are going to come and visit me next Sunday."

"Yes," said Rose happily. "I'm looking forward to going to the seaside properly. I don't think I saw it at its best on my first visit. I couldn't quite see the charm."

Thomas turned to Edward, who had been very quiet since events in the church. "After the station, we can drop you and Aurora at Silver Square, Edward."

Edward looked questioningly at his daughter, who flashed him an encouraging smile. "Actually, no. I don't think so, Thomas. If it's all right with you, I think Rory and I will come back to Campion's with you all. Rory and I have been talking – we think we'd like to move into Campion's on a permanent basis. We reckon that like all actors and performers, we're rogues and vagabonds at heart. We're not cut out to be lords and ladies."

"No," said Rory. "Being a lady is horribly dull

and much harder work than it looks."

"Does that mean," asked Rose, "that we can put the bicycle act back on the bill tonight?"

Aurora grinned and nodded. "But only if we're top of the bill," she said with a laugh.

"Well, actually," said Effie, "I was hoping for top of the bill for my debut tonight as the Fantastical Effie Madley, the Girl Conjuror."

They all stared at her open-mouthed.

"Are you quite sure you want to do a solo magic act, Effie?" asked Thomas.

"Yes," said Effie. "But I don't want to overreach myself so maybe I'll start at the bottom of the bill and work my way up. I need to remember everything that Mr Gandini taught me, and read as much about magic as I can so I get better. I'll do it for him as a memorial to his kindness to me." She paused. "Then, when I'm rich and celebrated as the world's most famous magician, I'll buy the Doomstone."

The others stared, open-mouthed and completely horrified. Effie burst out laughing at their faces.

"I'm only joking. I wouldn't touch the bloomin' thing. I've told you before, it's cursed."

Rose grinned and put her arm through Effie's,

and Aurora did the same. The three of them skipped down the road together, away from the glowering prison, and they didn't look back.

Look out for the first title in
Lyn Gardner's *Olivia* series:

Olivia's
First Term

LYN GARDNER

Turn the page for a sneak peek!

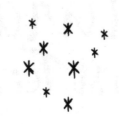

Chapter One

Olivia Marvell stood on the pavement in the pouring London rain. She screwed up her eyes as she lifted her face to the sky and the rain lashed down so hard it was like hundreds of tiny pinpricks. Olivia sighed. Even the weather had a grudge against her. She glanced at her dad, Jack, who since they had left the Tube station had been wrestling with an umbrella that kept being caught by the wind and turning itself inside out. The umbrella was clearly going to win. Jack looked as cold, wet and miserable on the outside as Olivia felt inside. She shivered. She hated London already; she had only been here for a few hours, and longed for the Italian late-summer sunshine that made you want to arch your back and stretch like a cat.

In one hand Olivia held a battered, bulging suitcase out of which poked a sodden, slightly muddy pyjama leg and the end of a thick wire; in the other she was holding the hand of Eel, her little sister. Eel hadn't been christened Eel, of course, but had acquired the nickname soon after birth because she was such a wriggly little thing, never still for a minute. She was jiggling around now, pulling on Olivia's hand, but Olivia only held on tighter.

"Cut it out, Eel! Anyone would think you were seven months old, not seven years," said Olivia irritably.

A few passers-by eyed them curiously, and one smartly dressed woman crossed over the road as if to avoid the raggle-taggle group.

"Bet she thinks that we're going to beg for money or mug her," muttered Olivia fiercely.

"You can't blame her," said Eel sadly, shaking her chestnut curls like a dog and spraying Olivia's face with more water. "We look rubbish. We probably pong too," she said, sniffing herself like a bloodhound. She was wrong about that, but they did look a mess. Olivia's hair was stuck damply to her face while Eel had a big smudge on her forehead and her skirt was torn after an unfortunate encounter with the ticket barriers at the Tube station. Eel had never seen ticket barriers before and had decided she never wanted to see them again. They had appeared determined to gobble her up.

"Come on, girls," said Jack, abandoning his tussle with the umbrella. "We'll be soaked through if we stand here any longer. Let's just walk fast. It's not very far." They set off at a brisk pace, even though it made Jack limp badly, and as they turned the corner of the street, an imposing red-brick building came into view. At the front of the building a sign written in large black letters declared "The Swan Academy of Theatre and Dance". In smaller letters below it said "An academic and performing arts education for talented children aged 7–16". Underneath that was written in italics: *"Proprietor: Alicia Swan"*.

"Here we are," said Jack, coming to a halt opposite the building and dragging them into a shop doorway for shelter.

Olivia's mouth fell open as she read the sign, and then she turned to her father and said accusingly, "It's a *stage* school. You said that we were going to stay with our grandmother and go to her school. You didn't tell us that she runs a *stage school*." Olivia spat out the words "stage school" as if they had a nasty taste.

Jack looked like a small boy who had just been caught with his fingers in the sweet jar. "Didn't I? I must have forgotten to mention it."

Olivia glared at him. "But you've always said that you hate all that fake theatre stuff, and so do we."

"Not me," piped up Eel. "I've always wanted to learn to dance but we've never stayed anywhere long enough to have lessons." She tried to do a little twirl and got tangled up with Olivia, who was still gripping her hand. "I'll be a great dancer. The bestest."

"You can't say bestest," said Olivia witheringly.

"I can if I want," said Eel, but she looked as if she might cry.

"I'm sure you'll be a fantastic dancer," said Jack soothingly, but Olivia detected a note of false cheerfulness in his tone.

"But what about me?" demanded Olivia. "I can't dance and I won't dance, and I don't want to go to stage school either. I want to stay with you and carry on walking the high-wire.

I'm a circus artist, not a stage-school brat."

Jack looked at his elder daughter, at her determined mouth and flashing eyes, and for a moment thought that his beloved wife, Toni, had suddenly come back to life. He shook his head sadly before swallowing hard and declaring a little too heartily, "Well, there is a choice. It's stage school or the orphanage run by a wicked old witch who eats children for breakfast."

"Well, I vote for stage school," said Eel, hopping from one leg to another, "and Livy will have to come too because she's superglued herself to me and is holding my hand so hard it hurts."

"That's because you can't be trusted!" said Olivia, the words exploding out of her mouth like a stuck cork suddenly released from the neck of a bottle. "It's all your fault that we're in this situation. If you hadn't. . ." She tailed off as she saw Eel and Jack's faces, white with shock. Olivia's anger evaporated as quickly as it had materialised and she burst into loud, guilty tears.

"Oh Eel, I didn't mean it! I'm really, really sorry," she sobbed. "I know it was an accident. It's just everything feels so miserable, and I'm tired of pretending everything is all right when it's not."

Eel hugged her and said tearfully, "It's OK, Livy. But we've got to make the best of things." She moved her head close to Olivia's and whispered, "We've got to be as brave as llamas and very cheerful. For Dad's sake, cos he hardly ever smiles now."

"I think you mean lions, Eel. Llamas probably aren't that brave. But you're right, Dad is so sad and defeated all the time." And, as if somebody had turned on a hosepipe, Olivia's tears started flowing again.

"He looks just like my teddy bear looked after he accidentally got put in the washing machine on an extra-hot wash," replied Eel sadly. "If it was an accident," she added ominously.

"It's nobody's fault," said Jack firmly. "We've just had some bad luck, my lovelies, but our luck will change."

"Look," said Eel, sniffing and pointing at the sky, "it's changing already. It's stopped raining and the sun has come out. I might even dry out if Livy would only stop crying all over me." Olivia gave a wan smile and hiccupped. . .